Welcome to the wonderful world of

Regency Romance!

For a free short story and to listen to me read

the first chapter of all my other Regencies,

please go to my website:

https://romancenovelsbyglrobinson.com

or use your phone with the following QR code:

Thank you!

GL Robinson

A Perfect Match

and Other Stories

Regency Romances

By

GL Robinson

As always, in memory of my dear sister,

Francine.

With thanks to my Beta Readers,

who always tell me what they think.

And with special thanks to CS

for his patient editing and technical help,

and more especially, his friendship.

Cover art: Hans Zatzka, Austrian 1855-1945

Contents

A Perfect Match

1

Chloë Purchase stood in the shadow of the long drapery and watched. Her quarry had been in the card room for what seemed like ages. Surely he would put in an appearance soon! She had been keeping an eye on the door most of the evening, steadfastly refusing any offers to sign her dance card.

"I've hurt my ankle," she smiled beguilingly up into the faces of would-be partners. "I'm afraid I can't dance at all this evening. I did it getting down from the carriage. So silly of me. I suppose I should have gone home, but I did so want to come."

Then, when they showed an inclination to linger at her side, she would say, "Look! Miss Dawson, or Petty, or Turnbull …," or any other maiden unfortunate enough to be without a partner as the fiddlers struck up, "is without a partner. It would be a kindness in you to ask her. And kindness is *so* important, don't you think? I could never like a man who wasn't kind."

What gentleman could bear the idea that those big blue eyes might not look fondly upon him if he showed himself unkind? One by one they left to do her bidding, leaving her free to once again fix her attention on the door from which the one man she was interested in maddeningly refused to emerge.

"I think I shall just try to walk around the room," she said finally to her duenna who sat, tapping her feet in time to the music. "No, don't get up, dear Moira. I know how much you like to watch the dancers. But I feel my ankle will seize up if I do not move it just a little."

With a seeming limp she took herself off and had now been standing here for what seemed like an age waiting for him to show himself. Luckily, the dance floor was so full Moira would not be able to see her.

She had a sudden thought and, withdrawing her pencil from the silver reticule on her arm, scrawled a number of illegible names in the spaces for all the dances except the remaining waltz. Then, at last, her patience was rewarded. She heard his deep baritone voice before she saw him, and she began to move towards the card room door, apparently deep in the contemplation of her dance card.

Sure enough, pushing his friend ahead of him with a laugh, Lord Gregory Sheridan emerged saying in his rumbling baritone, "Get along, do, Bunny. They've run out of the Pomerol in here and if you don't get a move on there won't be any left in the dining room either."

He was talking to his friend, she was deep in her card. The inevitable collision ensued. With a shocked "Oh!" Miss Chloë Purchase dropped her reticule, her fan, and her dance card, and looked as if she herself might fall.

Lord Sheridan put out his arms to catch the tottering maiden. For a moment her world stood still as he held her, his strong arms around her, his masculine scent in her nose, her face an inch from his white silk waistcoat.

His deep voice recalled her to her to her senses. "Good God! What on earth …?"

She looked up into his face. Now, she knew she was an extraordinarily pretty girl and so far, no man she had bent that blue gaze upon had ever been proof against it. Lord Sheridan appeared to be no exception.

"Why!" he said, smiling down at her. "I see now I had no need to catch you. You are an angel. You would simply have taken wing and flown!" She could feel his deep voice reverberating in the chest so close to her own.

Chloë giggled. "How pretty! But indeed, sir, I should have fallen if you had not caught me. I was foolishly looking at my dance card to see who is to partner me for the next dance. But I think I dropped it. And my fan. And my reticule."

She had a pang of disappointment as her savior released her. "Allow me," he said, and swiftly bent to pick up her scattered belongings.

"Thank you," she replied, slipping her fan and reticule onto her wrists and opening up the dance card. "Oh! It's a waltz. And I have no partner! How vexing! I do love to waltz."

Lord Sheridan looked at her card. "That's odd," he remarked. "All the other dances appear to be taken — and by the same person. The hand is the same."

"Oh no," she replied sunnily. "It's my handwriting. I put it in myself so I can read it afterwards. Some gentlemen, you know, make their letters so badly I cannot understand them."

"Hmm," he said, giving it back to her. "I'm glad you can read it. I certainly can't. But I should make myself known to you." He bowed, "Gregory Sheridan, at your service."

She curtseyed. "Chloë Purchase. I'm pleased to meet you, sir, and thank you again for catching me."

"Believe me, I count it a blessing. But now we are acquainted, perhaps you would allow me to dance the waltz with you. Since you strangely have no partner. And since you love to waltz."

"Oh, that would be so kind! I hope I don't tread on your toes. I'm not very expert, you know."

"Even if you do, I shall feel nothing. I believe angels are weightless creatures."

She giggled again. "Perhaps, but as a mere mortal I most definitely weigh something!"

"We shall see."

With that, he swept her away, leaving his friend Bunny, who had witnessed the whole exchange, shaking his head in surprise. Now that was a turn up for the books. Greg rarely danced, and never with hopeful maidens. What was the old boy up to?

The swains who had been refused earlier in the evening were astonished when they saw her twirling around the room with Gregory Sheridan. Her ankle seemed entirely healed. But then they saw that because of the disparity in their heights, her feet were barely touching the ground. That must be it. He must have asked her and she'd taken pity on the fellow. He had to be forty if he was a day. So they swallowed their disappointment and determined to ask her again after the break for supper.

But after supper she was gone. When discreet inquiries were made of the hostess, it was revealed the poor child had gone home early. The waltz with Lord Sheridan had aggravated her ankle. He had left too, gone off with Bunny Witherspoon probably to some hell somewhere. Really, one didn't know why one invited that set at all. They arrived late, left early and hardly ever danced. It was just that they were so rich, so well-known and so charming, one could never exclude them.

2

Chloë drummed her fingers on the table in irritation! A week! It had been a week since she had danced with Gregory Sheridan at that party. She had wasted half the evening waiting for him; she had denied herself the pleasure of dancing all the sets and she had left early to perpetuate the fiction of the sprained ankle. Had he even left his card? No. Had he been loitering in the street when she left the house in hopes of seeing her? No. Had he sent her so much as a flower? No. No, and No. For all the notice he had taken of her she might as well be invisible. For a maiden used to constant attention, this was more than a shock. It was a downright insult!

But she was not a girl to give up once she had set her mind on something. And she had set her mind on Gregory Sheridan. He was at least twenty years older than she, of course, but she found him *so* attractive! That deep voice! That powerful physique! He made all the younger men look like boys! From the first moment she'd seen him two weeks ago at the Chilterns' rout, she'd been determined to have him.

The problem was, he paid no attention to her or any other woman. He seemed interested only in sports. The *on dit* had it that he was an intrepid rider to hounds, a fearless participant in carriage races, an excellent shot, and preferred boxing to the more gentlemanly pursuit of fencing. He was certainly very strong. The way he had literally swept her off her feet during that dance had intoxicated her. She'd been able to think of nothing else this last se'ennight.

She had been sure he would have at least *tried* to see her again. Every other man of her acquaintance always had. Her guardian pretended to be stuffy about it, but if an admirer bearing a posy of violets asked to be allowed the favor of a few minutes speech with Miss Purchase, as he had something particular he wished to say, Fremont the butler would usually show him in. To be sure, the drawing room door would be left open and Moira Arthur, her duenna, would always be there, knitting or tatting or sewing or doing some other boring thing. But she was far from being closeted so closely no gentleman could even kiss her hand. Now the one gentleman she *wanted* to kiss her hand had shown absolutely no inclination to do so. It was maddening! Something Had To Be Done!

It wasn't long before she hit upon the Something. Casually entering the library where her guardian Lord Spotsford spent his days, she kissed him on the cheek and said, "Uncle dearest, where is Debrett's Peerage? Moira and I were discussing whether the English or Irish peerages were the older. I'd like to check."

This was, of course, complete fiction. Moira Arthur was the middle-aged daughter of an impoverished parson and had no more knowledge or care about the peerage in England, Ireland, or Timbuktu, come to that, than the man in the moon. She liked to watch ladies dancing with their lovely gowns and jewels, but she was a simple soul. She did not yearn after position or finery. Her idea of luxury was a warm fire and a hot toasted muffin with as much butter as she wanted, both of which had been conspicuously lacking in her youth.

"Hmm?" Her uncle looked up from the tome he was reading. The Peerage you say? I think you'll find the English titles are the older, though I believe that of the Duke of Ireland is quite ancient. Why do you wish to know?"

"Oh, just curiosity, Uncle."

"Pity. I was hoping you might be looking up the Duke of Grafton. Young Fitzroy has written again asking to pay you his addresses and he stands to inherit the title, you know."

"I do know but I don't care. I don't want Jack Fitzroy. He's just a boy. I declare, he's younger than I am!"

"That is not so, as I've told you before. But I am far from wanting to push you into an unwanted marriage, no matter how illustrious the groom's family."

"So, Uncle, the Peerage, where is it?" Chloë stared vaguely around the library. It must be said, she had not spent a great deal of time in there, the study of books not being much to her liking.

Her uncle rose to his feet and quickly found the volume, which he handed to his ward. "There you are. Just bring it back when you're finished with it. Don't leave it lying around the house like your tippets, your prayer book and the gloves I'm constantly finding everywhere."

"Of course not, Uncle dear," she said, and stood on tiptoe to kiss him on the cheek.

He patted her arm. "You're a good girl, but I pity your husband. You're right, young Fitzroy isn't the one for you. You need someone stronger."

"And older," said Chloë as she skipped from the library.

She used the Peerage to such advantage that the following morning at about eleven she was walking slowly down a particular street in Mayfair with her duenna, covertly looking at the numbers on the doors. Suddenly she stumbled and let out a cry. "My ankle! I've hurt it again!" She looked down at her foot. "No wonder! Look! The heel of my shoe has nearly come off! However did that happen?" She tried to step forward, but it was clearly impossible. "Oh, Moira! We'll simply have to knock on this door and see if someone can help."

"We could hail a hackney?" suggested the practical Moira.

"But my ankle is swelling again. I can feel it! I need a bandage or something. I can't go home like this!" She looked down. "How irritating! I was so enjoying our walk!"

"I'm astonished at that, Miss Purchase. There's nothing very interesting in looking at rows of houses. I was surprised you chose that instead of the park, to tell you the truth."

But Miss Purchase wasn't listening. She had vigorously pulled the bell of the nearest shiny black door and it was even now being opened by a sober gentleman whose attire proclaimed him the butler.

"I'm so sorry to bother you. My name is Chloë Purchase. I wonder if you can help me? The heel has come off my shoe and caused me to twist my ankle. I find I cannot walk."

Without waiting for an answer, she pushed the door open and, with surprising alacrity for one suffering from a twisted ankle, hobbled into the wide foyer. But as her foot hit the smooth black and white checked marble floor, the broken shoe slid forward at an awkward angle and caused her to give a loud cry.

A tall, broad gentleman surged from one of the doorways giving onto the foyer.

"What on earth ... Miss Purchase!"

"Lord Sheridan!"

Surprise on one side and satisfaction on the other appeared to rob them both of speech.

"My lord," said the butler, filling the silence. "The heel of Miss Purchase's shoe broke and caused her to twist her ankle. Our doorbell was the nearest to hand."

"How fortunate for us both!" said Gregory. He smiled down at his visitor, then, without a word, gathered her up and carried her through the doorway from which he had emerged. It proved to be an elegant drawing room. Moira Arthur scuttled in behind and perched herself on a chair in the corner.

"Allow me," said his lordship, depositing his burden gently on a fawn silk-covered sofa, "My goodness yes, the heel has almost come off. The nails must have somehow become loose. How odd."

He delicately removed the offending shoe and cradled Chloë's stockinged foot in the palm of one large hand. The warmth of it made her stomach lurch.

"Here, Wootton, take this downstairs and have someone see to it. And ask Mrs. Palmer to bring up a cold compress. The ankle is not yet much swollen and hopefully we can prevent it from becoming so."

His lordship stood up and went to a small table off to one side. It was crowded with bottles of all shapes and sizes and colors.

"Allow me to offer you some refreshment, Miss Purchase. I recommend a glass of wine for the shock."

Though she had drunk very little wine in her life and none at eleven in the morning, Chloë responded enthusiastically, "Oh, yes, please." Then, thinking that sounded too hearty for someone in pain, added in a fading voice, "I do feel a little faint."

His lordship poured a dark liquid into a small pretty glass and handed it to her. He turned to Moira. "May I offer you a glass too, Miss … er …? I think you will find it quite palatable."

"Miss Arthur, my lord. And no, no thank you," replied the duenna in a shocked voice. Nothing in the vicarage had prepared her for morning visits to single gentlemen, much less the drinking of spirituous liquors. If she had dared, she would have remonstrated with her charge, but Miss Purchase had looked at her with a set to her chin that Moira recognized. It would be useless.

Chloë sipped the wine. It was delicious. Sweet and smooth. She was preparing to drink it down and accept more when their host shocked her to the bottom of her soul.

"And now I must leave you," he said. "Unfortunately I have an engagement I cannot miss. My housekeeper will be here presently with a compress and someone will repair your shoe sufficiently to allow you to wear it home. Please stay as long as you need. My household is entirely at your service. I shall tell Wootton to have a carriage ready when you choose to depart. It was a pleasure to see you again, Miss Purchase, even under such, er, unfortunate circumstances."

He bowed to the ladies and was gone. They heard him exchange a few words with the butler, then there was the sound of the front door opening and closing.

"Well!" said Miss Purchase, her expression as close to a scowl as her lovely face would permit.

3

Two weeks passed and Miss Purchase saw and heard no more of Lord Sheridan than his back disappearing through a doorway, or the sound of his deep voice resonating from the masculine enclaves of the smoking or card rooms in the homes to which they had been invited. She had sent him a very pretty note thanking him for his services in the matter of the broken shoe but had received in return nothing more than his printed card with the words *Happy to have been of service* scrawled on it. She had stared at it in disbelief for a minute or two and almost tore it up in frustration, but her heart wouldn't let her. She ended up putting it in the book of devotions next to her bed. She opened the book every night, not, it must be said, to consider the works of the Almighty, but to gaze upon the card and imagine it being printed not with *The Lord Sheridan*, but with *Lord and Lady Sheridan,* herself featuring in the second role.

Now the season was drawing to a close and Chloe was faced with a dilemma. She had either to accept one of the numerous proposals of marriage her guardian had received on her behalf, or face the shocking possibility of entering her second season with no ring on her finger. Neither appealed to her.

But she was not a girl to give up so easily. She had taken to scouring the Court and Social news every day and was thus able to ascertain that Lord Sheridan was planning a visit to his estates in Buckinghamshire. He would consequently be away from the capital for the rest of the month.

"Doesn't Aunt Aurora live near Aylesbury in Buckinghamshire?" she asked her guardian. "I haven't seen her in an age. I think I'll write and invite myself for a fortnight. You don't mind, do you? I'll take the old carriage so you won't feel the lack of your new one."

Her uncle looked at her doubtfully. "Aurora? Yes, but she lives very quietly. I can't imagine what you'll do there. You'll be moped to death!"

"No I won't, Uncle! I love the countryside! I can go for long rambles. It will be delightful. I'm beginning to find the London salons such a bore!"

"In that case, go with my blessing. She'll be pleased to see you, I daresay. You are the image of our dear sister. Don't be surprised if she weeps over you. She always was a watering pot. But you needn't take the old carriage. I can manage with it for a fortnight. Or I can always take a hackney."

"Nonsense! I should be distressed to think of you being shaken about in that old thing, all because of me. It will carry Moira and me very well, don't worry."

Chloë had good reasons for wanting the old carriage, and when Moira gently complained about the rackety ride chided her. "You wouldn't want poor Uncle to have to use it, would you? I can't imagine what it would do to his old bones."

Since Moira herself was only a few years younger than Chloë's guardian, she could have complained about her own bones, but, being a patient soul, she refrained.

A week or so later saw Miss Purchase ensconced in her aunt's old house close to Aylesbury. No doubt an historian would have found much to recommend it. It dated from before the Civil War and had reputedly been a gathering place of the anti-Monarchist Roundheads. Chloë found it dark, damp, and drear. She wouldn't have been surprised to meet a ghost roaming the halls. As a modern Miss, she had no fear of ghosts and might even have enjoyed the experience. It would have been a change from the dreadfully dull evenings she spent with her aunt. They played interminable games of loo for miniscule stakes and then took turns reading aloud from Fordyce's Sermons.

The weather was fine, but the long rambles on foot did not materialize. Instead Chloë and Moira took a number of afternoon carriage rides. Mysteriously, they would often end up on the same road, driving past a fine-looking modern building, or, at least, it was a good deal more modern than her aunt's gothic pile.

"Whose is that house one passes on the road into town? The one with the white stone front," asked Chloë, fairly sure she knew the answer. Apart from *The Peerage*, the library at home had offered her other sources of information. She had found a very handy tome entitled *Fine Homes of England* in which Sheridan Place, just outside Aylesbury, was actually depicted. "It's amazing," she said to herself, "I never knew books could be so useful!" The author had given the additional information that Sheridan Place was believed to be designed by Inigo Jones. But since she had never heard of Mr. Jones, she ignored that tidbit.

"Oh, that! That's the Sheridan family home," said her aunt. "Such a pity. The old Tudor house burned down and they built that place in its stead. So shockingly white, I always think."

"I like it," said Chloë defensively. "It looks fine on the rise like that."

"Hmph!" responded her aunt.

A couple of days later Miss Purchase arrayed herself in her best riding costume of fine blue wool exactly the color of her eyes and trimmed with silver braid, donned her best bonnet, and walked into the drawing room. There, her duenna and her hostess were involved in the difficult and heavy task of repairing the hems of the drawing room curtains. According to Aunt Aurora, they had been made a shade too long (she'd said so at the time) and with constant rubbing on the floor had become worn into threads. Chloë announced she was taking a drive.

"But I can't leave this job with the curtains all over the drawing room floor!" protested Moira, "and it's going to rain!"

"Nonsense!" retorted Chloë. "Why should it rain? It's been fine all week! I don't wish to remain cooped up here, and you know I'm hopeless with a needle." This was true. Nothing her governesses had ever done had made her able to even sew on a button without pricking herself twenty times and bleeding all over the garment. "And I can perfectly well go alone. This isn't London. The streets are not unsafe. Besides, I'll have Thomas drive. He's young and strong. He'll protect me. You stay here and help Aunt with the curtains. It's a much more important task."

Before anyone could say anything more, she ran into the hall, caught up the bandboxes she had secreted in the cupboard there, and sped to the stables. Thomas was there, sweeping the floor. Luckily, he was alone.

"I'm expected at a friend's house for a few days," she told him. "My duenna is indisposed so I'm going by myself. Aunt Aurora says you're to take me as you're young and strong enough to protect me, if need be. Pole up my uncle's old carriage at once."

Young Thomas looked at her with his mouth open. She was a vision of loveliness in her new poke bonnet with the curling blue feather. No one had told him he was to drive her anywhere, but that was forgotten as he nodded in a daze. Yes, he would protect her though the devil himself were after them.

With Chloë tapping her foot with impatience, he poled the horses to the old carriage, helped the vision into it, and before long they were sedately clip-clopping out of the gates. Then he drew in the horses.

"Where be we a-goin', Miss?" he said, realizing he had no idea of their destination.

"Just go straight down the road into town and I'll tell you when you need to turn. I'll knock with my parasol once if I want you to stop, but I'm already late and I may need you to spring the horses. I'll knock twice if I do."

"Once to stop and twice to spring 'em," he repeated dutifully.

"Yes." She gave him her brilliant smile, and he needed no more bidding.

To Chloë's intense satisfaction, as they drove sedately down the road the sky darkened and before long a few drops of rain began to fall. This was exactly what she had been hoping for. As they came to what she guessed to be about two miles of the Sheridan home, she tapped sharply on the roof of the carriage with the handle of her parasol. The horses began to canter. A mile on, she tapped imperatively again and they went into a full gallop. The old vehicle bounced and rocked. She had to hang on for dear life. By now the rain was coming down in sheets. She knew that just before the gates of the house there was a sharp turn in the road. She was counting on that, together with the poor visibility and the speed of travel, to cause some sort of accident.

In plotting this daring last move in her pursuit of Gregory Sheridan, she had thrown all caution to the winds. The possibility of injury to herself or anything else was the last thing on her mind as the white house came into view through the driving rain. She clung onto the straps and closed her eyes. There was a wild swerve; she heard a loud "Woah, there, woah!" and the crazy gallop slowed. Suddenly, there was a loud crack, the carriage tilted crazily to one side and came to a complete halt. A wheel had broken clean off.

Chloë opened her eyes. Her bandboxes and parasol had slid to the downside of the carriage. She was still clinging, high up at the other end.

"Miss! Miss! Be you all right?" First Thomas's voice, then his whole head came through the window on the down side. "If I gets this 'ere door open, can you slide down?"

"Yes, I think so. I'm not injured. What about you and the horses?"

"I'm fine. The 'orses too. Lucky I pulled 'em in afore the wheel broke. They're standin' yonder as nice as yer please."

"Get that door open if you can, then turn away. I'm going to slide down."

Chloë let go of the straps, lowered herself to the floor of the carriage, wrapped her skirts firmly round her ankles and, holding them tight with one hand, bumped her derrière down to the other end. She could see Thomas's back as he stood outside keeping the door open. Her bandboxes were on the grass verge beyond. She pushed her feet through the door until she could put them down, then let go of her skirt and stood up.

"Thank you, Thomas. You are a gentleman."

Chloë walked on shaky legs to the front of the carriage. It was slumped to one side, but miraculously in one piece, the broken wheel on the ground. It was drizzling, but the heavy rain had ceased. The horses were peaceably cropping at the grass verge. She turned and looked up the road. The tall iron gates to Sheridan Place stood open.

"I shall take my boxes and go up to that house," she announced. "You unhitch the horses and walk them. They will take cold if they stand like that after such a gallop. I shall send someone to help you as soon as I can."

If young Thomas had been more experienced or quicker thinking, he might have suggested putting Miss Purchase on one of the horses and walking her, with the other horse behind, up to the house. But he was in the habit of taking orders and simply nodded. "Yes, Miss."

Chloë picked up her bandboxes and began to walk towards the gates. She soon found that carrying the boxes was no mean feat. They were heavy for they contained, besides night clothing and hair and tooth brushes, a lovely evening gown and slippers, her best Norwich silk shawl, and her newest day dress. Adding to her discomfort, the kid booties that so admirably matched her riding suit were new and pinched her toes quite dreadfully.

Then it started to rain again, and the path rose inexorably upwards. When Inigo Jones had designed the house, he had set it on an elevation, intending it to appear between the trees as one rode up to it. He had not imagined a dripping, tired, footsore, and overburdened young lady. Chloë was almost in tears by the time she arrived at the great front door. Her arms felt wrenched from their sockets, the poke of her bonnet had collapsed and the feather was in her eyes, her boots were drenched and her waterlogged wool skirt was dragging her down. She pulled the big bell handle and heard it ring somewhere deep inside.

To her surprise, the door was opened by Gregory Sheridan himself. He was calling over his shoulder to someone, the butler presumably, "Don't worry, Timpson. I'll get it. I'm right here."

When his eyes fell on his visitor they opened wide with, what was it? Amusement. Yes, that's what it was. His lordship looked amused. Chloë's tearfulness immediately transformed into fury. Her blue eyes flashed. "I don't see anything funny about it. The wheel came off my carriage in the road by your gate and I have walked what must be ten miles uphill with these heavy bandboxes. I'm tired and wet and if you don't let me in I shall stand here and scream!"

It was hard for Gregory to control himself. These fighting words coming from a maiden whose bonnet was hanging limply by the sides of her head, whose skirts were inches deep in mud and whose face bore large smear of dirt on one cheek almost overcame him.

"Good gracious," he said, his voice trembling. "First your heel, then your wheel. You do seem unlucky with your means of conveyance."

Her eyes flashed dangerously, and he held out his hand. "But, where are my manners? Please come in, Miss Purchase. Here, give me those bandboxes. Good lord, what's in them? Your whole wardrobe?"

He pushed her towards an open door. Beyond it, she could see a welcome fire blazing. She went in and stood in front of it. She undid the ribbons of her bonnet and pulled off her sodden gloves, then looked for someone to take them.

"I'm sorry. the staff are having their tea and you may have heard me tell my butler to stay where he was. Allow me." He took the offending articles and placed them on a table off to one side.

Suddenly, Chloë was overcome with the enormity of what she had done. Here she was, alone in his home with a gentleman, no servants in sight. It was what she had planned, of course. She had wanted to trap him so he would marry her, but now, now what was she to do? She was tired and wanted to sit down, but her clothes were so muddy she would ruin the furniture! She was cold and wet and had to take care of Thomas and the horses, when all she wanted was someone to take care of her! And he … he was laughing at her! She sank to her knees in front of the fire and burst into tears.

His lordship looked at her and slowly shook his head. He took a blanket off the back of a chair and put it around her shoulders. Then he went to a side table and poured something into a glass. He bent to put it in her hands.

"Here, drink this while I go to tell someone to fetch your driver and the horses. I imagine they are still waiting?"

She nodded miserably and sipped her drink. It was the same thing he had given her in London. It was wonderfully warming. She sat down fully, stretched her feet towards the fire and looked around. She was in a library. The tall windows looked west. It had stopped raining and a weak late afternoon sun was just emerging from behind barred clouds. Its rays shone pale gold on the panes in the glass-fronted bookcases, on the dark wood furniture, on the Turkish carpet where she was sitting. Chloë had left her reticule with her parasol in the carriage and had no handkerchief.

She wiped her eyes with the back of her hand and it came back smudged with dirt. Did she have dirt on her face? She hastily pulled up her skirt and lifted her petticoat to her face to wipe it.

Gregory Sheridan, coming back into the room, beheld the lovely girl sitting in a pool of sunshine, her golden curls falling down her back, her skirt to her knees, mopping her face with her lace-trimmed petticoat. He went out again, coughed loudly and came back in. Miss Purchase was still on the floor, but sitting up primly, her hands folded in her lap.

She looked up at him. "I'm sorry to be sitting on the floor, but I'm so muddy, I'd spoil your ... things."

"My things can think of nothing better than to be spoiled by you," he said gently. But he sat down next to her on the floor. "Suppose you tell me the whole story."

She was too discouraged to dissemble. "Oh, I think you've guessed it already. My plan was to have you compromise me so that you'd feel honor bound to marry me."

"And the broken heel and the dropped dance card?"

"To make you notice me. I thought if you noticed me, you'd want to marry me." She smiled sadly. "All the others have, you see."

"Yes, well, it worked. I did notice you. Dropping the dance card could have been an accident, but having all the dances except the waltz filled in with the same hand was a little hard to swallow. And the marks made on the broken heel of your shoe by, what was it? A knife? To loosen it?"

She nodded. "I'm sorry."

"Don't be. I have to confess I've been playing a game of my own. I was looking forward to seeing what you would do next. I thought you a woman of infinite resource. I wondered if you would pursue me here, and you didn't disappoint me. This has been your best effort yet. But, Miss Chloë Purchase, if you wanted so much to marry me that you'd compromise yourself, why didn't you just ask me?"

She looked at him in astonishment. "What do you mean? *I* ask you to marry *me*?"

"Yes. Why not? You are a modern woman. You have already exercised the right to choose a husband, it's only a step further to ask him to marry you."

She looked at him shyly, "But would he accept me?"

"You will have to ask him to see."

She thought for a moment, then set her chin in the way Moira would have recognized. Gathering her wet skirts, she struggled up to her knees and turned to face him.

"Lord Gregory Sheridan, will you marry me?"

He too rose to his knees. "Yes, Miss Chloë Purchase, yes, with all my heart, I will."

"Really? Oh, thank goodness!" Chloë launched herself at him. He laughed and caught her. Then he kissed her. It was all she had imagined it would be, and more.

When they finally broke apart, Gregory pulled her to her feet and said, "Now come and meet my sister. I've told her about you and she's looking forward to seeing you."

"Your sister?"

"Yes, she lives here. She doesn't care for the city."

"You mean she's been here all along? I wasn't going to compromise myself?"

"I'm afraid not."

"Gregory Sheridan, you tricked me!"

"Let's say we tricked each other. A perfect match, don't you think?"

"Yes," she said and smiled up at him. "A perfect match."

The End

Juliet and Romeo

1

"Well, that's that," said Emmet Waltham to his sister. He plumped himself next to her on the sofa. "Old Arnold's gone, finally. That's the trouble when one's lawyer has known everyone in the family for the past three generations. He can't shut up."

"I thought he did a very nice job of reading the Will," said Juliet mildly. "And he was very respectful to you."

"Hmpf! When everyone was listening. But afterwards he pulled me aside and prosed on about settling down, finding a nice girl, setting up my nursery ... you know, the old stuff. As if I hadn't heard it a thousand times from Papa."

"Well, now you're the Earl, I suppose it's your duty to do that." Juliet looked at him. She knew he had stubbornly refused all representations to put himself under the cat's paw, as he termed it. But his response surprised her.

"Funny you should say that say that, Etty. After all, when I get married my wife will want you and Mama shuffled off to the Dower House. You'll spend the rest of your days in that gloomy place."

"The Dower House? The rest of my days?"

"Yes. It's not as if you're ever going to marry. The one Season in London didn't see you off and Papa refused to put up the blunt for a second. Too late now. Anyway, you'll be needed as a Prop to Mama in her old age."

Something like an icicle stole into Juliet's heart. She had never heard it put so baldly, but now she thought about it, she supposed that *was* what life held in store. She stole a look round the familiar room with its tall windows and comfortable furniture. She had lived at Waltham Place all her life. She'd been born there. Apart from the one horrible Season in London, she'd never slept anywhere else. Well, except for the posting houses on the way to the capital.

She knew the Dower House, of course. It was on the other side of the park. She used to go there with her mother to visit her grandmama. Her abiding memory was the fusty smell of rooms not sufficiently aired and the ointment her grandmother applied to her joints every day. The house had been closed up since her grandmother died. It was probably damp and she was sure it would still smell. But, as Emmet said, that was probably where she'd end up.

She sighed in acquiescence. "I suppose you're right. But you will let me come and visit, won't you?"

"Lord, yes! We'll need you here too. The Missus and I won't want to be stuck here all the time. You can look after the children while we're gone. When you're not being a Prop to Mama."

She reflected wryly that at least she wouldn't be without employment.

Juliet was mild and biddable by temperament and had always done what everyone told her. Except find a husband. She had received one offer and Papa had been delighted. But she couldn't, she really couldn't! He was too old! His chin had grey bristles and he smelled! He had partnered her in a few country dances and she'd had to hold her breath when the movement called for them to hold each other. And that had been at arm's length! Thank God he didn't waltz!

That was the only time she'd ever defied her father and she'd never been allowed to forget it. Her father had refused to finance a second season, not that she wanted one. Almost the last thing he had said to her before he died was, "Don't forget you gave up the opportunity to be mistress of your own establishment. You'll end up an old maid and you've no one to blame but yourself. You're lucky I didn't send you to live with your Aunt Prudence. Two old biddies together!"

So she had learned not to complain, and no doubt when she was forced to go to the Dower House, she wouldn't complain then either.

2

The new Earl didn't seem any more inclined to listen to his lawyer than he had his father. He disappeared for months at a time to London and only reappeared when, as he put it, he needed to draw in the bustle a bit.

"Been dashed unlucky with the gee-gees," he'd say, or, "Damn shame Tufty grazed the wall going through that gate. I'd backed him to get though without a scratch. Seen him do it a thousand times. 'Course, he was always drunk then. He was sober this time. If I'd known, I'd have cried off!"

Their mother would sigh over his choice of friends and instruct cook to make all his favorite dishes. Juliet would sew up the rents in his shirts he seemed to acquire so easily.

"Don't know how that happened," he said once, coming upon her mending a great rip up the back of his shirt, "unless it was when I had to dive under the table that time. Girl's husband came home."

"Oh, Emmett, you didn't!"

"I damned well, er sorry, I dashed well did. You think I'd wait around for him to catch me? Great brute of a fellow he was!"

"I mean, you didn't, well, consort with that type of female? Aren't you looking for a nice girl to be your wife?"

"Yes, 'course I am, but you know, they aren't much fun. I mean, look at you! Perfect wife material, sewing, keeping the hearth warm and all that, but you're not much fun, are you?"

Juliet supposed he was right. She wasn't much fun. But really, how could she be? She'd been hemmed in by convention her whole life. From her first nursemaid to her last governess the precept had always been, "Act like a lady, not a hoyden. Gentlemen don't like *fast* women." And she always had. It was too late now. She would never be fun. Nor have any, come to that.

About a week after her brother's return to the City after his latest repairing lease, the weather was finally dry long enough for Juliet to consider taking a walk beyond the gravel path around the house. Yet another of the strictures she had absorbed growing up was to be careful not to get one's feet wet, because it invariably led to a chill, an inflammation of the lungs and certain death. So she waited prudently till the ground was no longer damp underfoot before going on a long walk with a new young dog Emmet had foisted on them.

Not that either Juliet or her mother had wanted another animal. Old Dido lazing in front of the fire suited them both. Her demands were few: a warm bed and a good dinner. But Emmet had bought this new young spaniel from yet another of his friends who had promised him it was a fine retriever. How could it not be? Its dam and its sire had been perfect: wonderful noses and soft mouths.

However, nature was evidently in a playful mood when this offspring was produced. On his first shoot, the young dog proved only one thing: it loved the water. It loved it so much that it couldn't wait for a bird to actually fall in before careering off at top speed with the maximum of bark and splash, oblivious to both the voice of its master and the need to retrieve anything.

"Damn thing cost me a good day's shooting," grumbled Emmet when he came home empty-handed and muddied all over from wrestling the dog from the lake. "Frimpton told me to get rid of it. Never be any good, he says. I suppose I'll have to put a bullet in its brains."

"Oh, don't do that," said his soft-hearted sister. She looked at the dog frolicking around the rose bushes massed in front of the house, chasing butterflies. "He seems such a cheerful soul."

Secretly she rather admired the animal. Unlike her, he had obviously paid no attention to any of the precepts his parents had tried to fix in his brain. He was a free spirit.

"Mama and I will have him indoors. He'll cheer us up when you're gone."

For although Emmet's intervals at home were always accompanied by groans about how money just seemed to go nowhere and complaints there was nothing to do in the country, his presence was always a welcome change at Waltham Place.

3

The dog, which in a flight of fancy Juliet named Aeolus after his ability to run like the wind and cause as much devastation, certainly did make a change in the placid home. He raced like a wild thing everywhere, chewed anything he could get his paws on and ate both his and old Dido's dinner, until the footman whose job it was to feed the dogs realized what was going on. After that, he locked him in the broom cupboard while Dido finished her leisurely meal. After his daily exertions, at night the puppy would fall into the deep sleep of the just, usually on Juliet's feet.

He clearly needed a good deal more exercise, so when the ground was dry enough not to cause the dreaded wet feet, inflammation of the lungs, etc. etc. she took him on a very long walk to the edge of their domain. The path she took followed the contour of the lake, but was high enough above it, however, to prevent Aeolus catching sight of the water. The lake extended beyond their property, and one of the strictures everyone in Waltham Place knew was that one did not venture beyond the Great Oak that marked the division between their land and their neighbors'.

The owners of The Park (as it was called) were the Brougham family, but they were never there. Lord Brougham had married a Frenchwoman who apparently preferred the delights of the Continent to the green leafiness of England. Consequently it was there he had made his home. Rumor had it that the lady was an ardent Pantheist. The word was only vaguely understood in that stolid Church of England enclave, but she was known to despise blood sports and to be of the opinion that nature should be left to its own devices. The gamekeeper evidently had strict instructions. He was ruthless in patrolling the land under his control and shot at anyone who dared venture there. He even refused to allow the hunt to follow Reynard onto the land.

The word was out amongst the furred, plumed-tail brethren and they all knew that to dash beyond the Great Oak was to dash into safety. As a result, the fox hunting in the neighborhood was poor: they often had to turn back. This was another reason for Emmet to bewail the lack of sport in the country.

Aeolus, of course, had never heard the strictures concerning the neighbors' land. Or if he had, he ignored them. With a bound, he flew beyond the Great Oak and could be heard crashing amongst the ferns. He could smell the foxes and was keen to have some fun with them. Juliet called and called for him to come to heel. It was useless. She might as well have called the wind for which he was named. So with enormous caution she stepped for the first time in her life beyond the Great Oak.

Having done so, she stood stock still, expecting some sort of cataclysm. It did not come. The birds, who had at first been shocked into twittering disarray by the advance of Aeolus, had now resumed their normal singing. The sun shone through the boughs of the big old trees and dappled the tops of the gently waving ferns. All was peace.

It would be nice to be able to say that Juliet walked boldly forward, but the habit of caution was so ingrained in her that a timid pace was all she could achieve. She could hear the dog smashing around in the ferns growing thickly on the slope that led down to the lake and she knew it was only a matter of time before the wretched animal found the water and threw himself into it.

The path she was on seemed to be descending towards the water, so she followed it and in a few minutes found herself on a sort of promontory overlooking the stony shore of the lake. The ground rose behind her but fell away in front. She could now see Aeolus's chestnut head bobbing up and down as he snuffled around. The ferns were as tall as he, so he had not yet observed the water. All might be well if only he would come when called!

"Aeolus! Come here at once," she called as sternly as she could looking down at the gamboling dog. When no response was forthcoming, she shouted in some temper, "You stupid animal! Aeolus, if you go into that lake, I'm leaving you there and going home!" This was the first time in her life she had ever cried out so loudly or uttered a threat of any kind. Her governesses would not have recognized her.

"*What* did you call him?" came a voice from behind her.

With a gasp of fear, Juliet whirled around and beheld the owner of the voice.

Coming towards her from the opposite direction was a slender man of average height. He wore tan wool britches with a long tailed tweed jacket over a moleskin waistcoat with a comfortable rather than elegantly-tied neckcloth. The outfit was completed by stout brogues, a beaver hat, and a blackthorn walking stick. Everything about him should have proclaimed an English gentleman in the country, but there was nonetheless something slightly foreign-looking about him. Was it because his hat was cocked on one side of his head, or the way he was twirling his walking stick? She didn't know, but her immediate reaction was that he, like her, was trespassing in someone else's woods. Her next thought was how nice-looking he was. Not really handsome, but open-faced and kind.

For the gentleman's part, he found himself looking at a rather undersized young woman, clad in a dull grey walking dress with matching pelisse. Neither was very fine and both showed distinct signs of wear: the hem of the dress and the cuffs of the pelisse were shredded. But her exertions had given color to her pale face, which was further enlivened by the scrap of lace around her collar. Her efforts had also caused her brown hair, drawn up in two wings under a serviceable felt bonnet, to begin to fall in gentle curls on her cheeks. His first thought was how nice looking she was. Not really beautiful, but open-faced and kind.

"I know I shouldn't be here!" she gasped. "But my dog ...."

"Neither should I," he said, "and I don't have the excuse of a dog. *What* did you say his name was?"

"Aeolus," she said. "Silly, I know, but he *is* like a whirlwind. Oh no! He's seen the lake! He'll be in it in a minute and I'll never get him out!"

They both looked down at the dog, who had indeed just realized there was a wide body of water in front of him. He barked at it once or twice, then since it gave no response, began to dart at the edges of the water.

Juliet's companion astonished her by taking a couple of long steps down the slope into the ferns and picking up a stout rope that in her concern over Aeolus she hadn't noticed. She saw now it was attached to a thick branch in one of the trees overhanging the path. Before she could utter a word, he had pulled the rope up with him to where the land rose behind them and then, coming forward at a run, he kicked off and, holding the rope, swung down to the shore of the lake. Aeolus lost his interest in the water and yelped at the body hurtling towards him. The gentleman put his feet down, ran a few steps and with one arm picked up the cowering animal. He then climbed up the slope back to Juliet, holding both the rope and the dog.

He deposited Aeolus at her feet where he sank down, quivering, and then dropped the rope. Fishing in his pocket, he drew out a length of string.

"Let's tie him to the trunk of the tree and take turns swinging."

"T-take turns sw-swinging?" Juliet couldn't believe her ears.

"Yes, I bet whoever put that rope there used it to plunge into the lake. Great fun! Pity we can't do that now!"

"G-great fun?" echoed Juliet doubtfully. Then a blinding realization hit her. This was IT. Emmet had just told her she was no fun. Well, this was the moment to prove him wrong. The chance might never come again.

"Yes," she said firmly. "Let's take turns swinging."

"Good girl! Let me go first to make sure the rope can take my weight again. We don't want it breaking and dropping you in the lake!"

"N …no," she said. "We don't."

Her companion swiftly tied Aeolus to the tree, picked up the rope and repeated the action from before. He climbed higher to begin and this time he flew out over the water, holding on as the rope swung back before dropping to the ground when it slowed half way up the slope.

"Your turn," he said, climbing up the rest of the way and handing her the end of the rope. "Have you done this before?"

"No, never," said Juliet in some trepidation.

"It's easy. Don't worry. I'll help you until you get the hang of it."

He led her not far up the rise behind them, much lower than where he had started from. "Try it from here. It probably won't go any further than the shore. You're very light. I'll give you a push to get you going. When you feel me push, pick up your feet."

Juliet tucked her skirts between her ankles, clutched the rope, oblivious of staining her gloves, closed her eyes and felt two strong hands on the small of her back. She picked up her feet and sailed through the air. The sensation took her breath away.

"Put your feet down now!" came the cry, and she did.

She felt herself being propelled forward on the stones by her own momentum and stumbled, but soon came to a halt. She opened her eyes. She was by the edge of the water. Then her companion was beside her.

"Good girl! You did it! Give me the rope, I'll take it back up. Come on!"

He helped her up the slope, then left her as he went even higher on the rise behind them and sailed way out over the water. He was laughing delightedly as he came back and handed her the rope. "That was the best yet! Your turn!"

This time she allowed herself to start a little higher up and when he gave her a push she kept her eyes open. It was exhilarating! Such freedom! She was flying like a bird! She felt a stab of alarm as she began to approach the water, but heard the cry "Put your feet down!" She did, and all was well.

"It was wonderful!" she said when he came down again to help her. "Even when I thought I was going out over the lake!"

Yes, I was so tempted to let go last time, and drop in," he replied. "But then I thought it wouldn't be fair as you couldn't do the same."

"No, indeed!" she said, but privately wished she could, just once, drop into the lake just to see what it felt like. Then she remembered. "I can't swim," she said ruefully.

"No, I didn't expect you could. Girls aren't encouraged to do that, are they? So silly, I think. If I had a daughter I'd make sure she could swim, and ride and even fence if she wanted to."

"I can ride," she said, a little defensively, but then her natural honestly asserted itself. "I'm not very brave though. Emmet, my brother, always says I should throw my heart over, but I can't. At least, I always think even if I could throw my heart over, the rest of me wouldn't follow!" They both laughed. Then Juliet said, "I hope your daughter, if you have one, is made of sterner stuff than I!"

He was about to say something when they heard a cry from the top of the slope behind them.

"Oy! What d'yer think yer doin' down there? Clear off!"

Juliet gasped. "It's the gamekeeper! The owners of this place don't like people trespassing. We'd better leave. I believe he would be within his rights to shoot us!"

"Shoot us? Is that the reputation the family has, then?" He looked at her a little strangely.

"Yes. We don't know them at all, but no one likes them, I'm afraid."

While she was talking she was untying the dog, who seemed inclined to want to lick her companion's shoes. "Come along, Aeolus. Quickly. I don't want that man to shoot you. Although it would serve you right if he did. You're the one that got us into this mess in the first place."

But even as she said it, she knew it hadn't been a mess. It had been the best moment of her life. She had had fun and she wouldn't give up a minute of it for a million pounds. She set off running back the way she had come and had already gone a hundred yards when she heard her companion cry out, "What's your name?"

"Juliet," she called back. "What's yours?"

"Romeo," he said, and laughed.

Juliet hugged her new experience to herself, telling no one but replaying it over and over in her mind. She smiled when she thought of him calling back "Romeo," like that. The answer had been perfectly right. She didn't need to know his real name. Their whole encounter had been a like a story. A dream. She would remember it the rest of her life: the feeling of flying over the ferns towards the shining water of the lake, his smiling face as he talked about having a daughter, his laugh.

The only part of it that hadn't seemed unreal was the feel of his hands in the small of her back. If she closed her eyes and thought about it, she could feel them again, warm and strong. She spent hours daydreaming about that moment, so much so that her mama, having twice asked a question and getting no response, asked if she were feeling quite well.

Aeolus didn't seem to agree with her about not knowing who the stranger was. He would pull her towards the path that led to the Great Oak and beyond, but Juliet refused to go there. She had been genuinely afraid of the gamekeeper, but more than that, she felt if she went back to that spot and he wasn't there, it would be spoiled forever. No, better just keep the perfect dream in her heart.

A couple of weeks later, Emmet sent his mother a rare letter.

Dear Mama,

You will never guess who I've met! Henry Brougham! Fine fellow! He's the son of our neighbors, the mad French ones, except he's not French at all. Well, he was born and brought up in Paris, but his Papa insisted on educating him at Harrow where he went himself. So he's as English as me. Not as good as if he'd gone to Eton, of course, but you can't have everything.

But the most amazing thing is, seems he's heard great things about Juliet. Juliet! I told him he must be mistaken, but he insists a friend of his who met her thought she was a regular out and outer. I don't know who it can have been, but anyway, seems he was smitten and now Henry wants to meet her.

So I'm bringing him home next week. He's going to be disappointed, of course. I've told him not to expect much, but you might try to get her to buck up a bit. Maybe wear a bit of paint, or whatever it is women do to make themselves attractive. Probably just as well he sees her and gets it out of his system. Then he can come back up here to find a wife. There's no shortage of lookers, that's for sure.

See you Tuesday se'ennight. For God's sake, Mama, spruce up Juliet so she's not an embarassment to us all!

Your loving son,
Emmet.

When her mother read her the salient parts of this missive, Juliet was dumbfounded. Who was this person she had supposedly so impressed he'd passed the memory onto Henry Brougham? And what kind of fool must this Henry be, to listen to any of that crowd? Her memory of her Season in London was of overdressed, simpering young women and empty-headed young men addicted to idiotic games.

"I think there's just time for Sally to run you up a new gown," said her mother. The last one didn't really suit you after all. That yellowish green is such a hard color to wear."

Juliet had told her mother precisely that when she proposed it, but her mother was, in her way, as stubborn as Emmet. Besides, they had had the length of that fabric in the house and it was a shame not to use it.

"If you think so, Mama. I should like something in a pale pink, if you don't object."

Her mother looked at her consideringly. "Hmm ... perhaps you're right. It might put some roses in your cheeks. I think I'll have Broome use just a touch of rouge." Broome was the Countess's long time dresser.

"Rouge, Mama? Oh, please, no! I should feel like a clown. Anyway, the minute he saw me, this Henry Brougham would know I was just a plain Jane pretending to be something else. He must be used to the beauties of Paris."

"Nonsense! You look a fresh English girl. Exactly what you are. There's no need to be ashamed of that. All you need is a bit of color."

In the event, Juliet did have a pale pink gown and it did bring color to her cheeks. She had absolutely refused to allow Broome to apply any rouge, but she let her arrange her hair becomingly, with curls falling over her ears. She also wore her grandmother's pearls. All in all, she looked, exactly as her mother had said, like a nice English girl.

She was alone in the drawing room when the tall windows showed her brother riding up the gravel drive with another man. There was something familiar about him, but the pillars of the portico obscured her view as they came closer. She heard talking in the hall and then steps approaching the door.

"If it's only Etty in there," came her brother's voice, "don't bother to announce us, Davidson. I can present my friend."

The door opened and Emmet walked in. To her utter astonishment, the man she knew as Romeo was close behind him.

"Juliet this is my friend ...," he began.

But she was already on her feet exclaiming, "It's you!"

"I'm afraid it is," he laughed. "Were you expecting someone else?"

"Yes. I was expecting Henry Brougham."

"I'm Romeo Henry Brougham. My mother's fancy, I'm afraid. She's a romantic and doesn't give a fig for English convention. I should have been Henry Brougham the Fourth. Better than Henry the Eighth, I suppose." He laughed again. "Thank God my father insisted on the middle name. You've no idea how much trouble I got into being called Romeo at Harrow."

"I should think so! Romeo indeed!" Emmet looked disgusted. "Good thing you never told me. I probably wouldn't have brought you home to meet my sister. Let's not tell mama. Where is she, by the way?"

"On her bed with a handkerchief soaked in lavender water on her forehead," said Juliet. "Her new gown was all wrong and she went into a decline."

"What stuff! I'll make her come down and meet Henry. Romeo! Good God!" Emmet stalked out of the room.

Romeo came to Juliet and clasped her hands. "I'd only just arrived at The Park that day. I'd never been there before and I decided to walk down to the lake. My father told me how he used to play there as a boy. The gamekeeper didn't know me, but you can be sure he pretty soon did! I was only there a couple of days trying to sort things out, then an urgent letter called me back to London. I'm coming to live here. I don't like cities, Paris or London. My father's handing The Park over to me and there were papers to sign. I didn't have time to try to find you. But you told me your brother's name was Emmet so I asked around town for someone of that name. It's not too common, thank goodness. I soon found him and made up that story about a friend being taken with you. I thought it was better than trying to explain the whole story with the swing and everything."

"Oh, yes," said Juliet. "I hardly believed it myself. I thought it was a dream. Except for ...," she broke off and blushed.

"For what?"

"For the wonderful feeling of you pushing me," replied Juliet, her face pinker than it had ever been in her life, but determined to tell the truth while she had the courage.

"Yes, it was wonderful," said Romeo softly and pressed her fingertips to his lips.

At that moment the door was pushed open by the chestnut head of Aeolus, who rushed in and joyfully tore around their visitor's feet before jumping up and putting his paws on his britches.

"Hello Aeolus!" said Romeo, giving the dog a pat. "I see you haven't learned any better manners."

"No," said Juliet, coming out of the reverie induced by having her fingertips kissed. "I'm afraid it's hopeless."

"We'll see," he replied, and looking at the dog, said firmly, "Aeolus! DOWN! NOW!"

To Juliet's astonishment, the dog immediately sat down, looking up at Romeo with adoration, his tongue hanging out.

"There you are then," said Romeo, looking her in the eyes. "We both find the memory of me pushing you wonderful and I seem to be the only person who can control this dog. There's nothing for it but for us to marry." He went down on one knee. "Will you, Juliet, do me the honor of becoming my wife?"

"Oh, yes, Romeo, I will. With all my heart, I will," she replied. "On condition that you teach me to swim, to fence, and perhaps even to box."

He laughed. "Of course! That goes without saying!"

And when her mother came in a few moments later, she found her gently-reared daughter being ruthlessly kissed by a complete stranger. She seemed to be enjoying it.

The End

The Consummate Diplomat

1

"I have sent for him to confirm this, but I assure you, Mr. Manchester, my son has no intention of marrying your daughter." The lady looked him up and down with a piercing eye. "It is impossible that she be allied with our House."

Mr. Manchester was unaccustomed to women of any age looking at him like that. He was tall, well-proportioned, still retained the flat stomach of his youth and had a good leg in a pair of britches. His hair was greying on the sides, but still sufficiently full to be brushed into a Brutus. He was generally held to be a handsome man looking much younger than his fifty years.

"And I assure *you*, Lady Westcott," he countered, "that my daughter would be an ornament to any House in the land. But I agree it is impossible she should be allied with yours."

He in turn looked at the lady. She was sitting bolt upright, her back perfectly straight, not touching an inch of her throne-like chair. He judged her to be all of forty. In fact, since her dratted son was twenty-five, she was almost certainly older. But he had to admit she had aged well. Her hair, which must once have been blond, was now more silver but still abundant and drawn up becomingly on the top of her head. She had a trim waist and a shapely ankle peeped out from beneath a fashionable gown of pale lavender silk with a froth of écru lace around the décolleté and elbow length sleeves. Mr. Manchester, an expert in women's apparel, not to mention women themselves, appreciated her good taste.

It was a stand-off. The lady and gentlemen glared at each other, neither willing to cede an iota. Suddenly the door to the salon opened and a good-looking though wispy youth entered, looking mutinous. He was of average height, but his extreme slimness made him appear taller. He had pale hair that showed a tendency to flop in his eyes, and he constantly pushed it away with an irritated hand.

"Ah, Roland, there you are," said the lady. "I sent for you because ...."

"Whatever the reason, Mama," he cried, "as I told Ruthven, I'm too busy to attend to it! I just began the final Act of my play and it's essential I finish it while I have the vision before me!"

"My dear boy, what I have to ask you is more important than your scribbling!"

"More important than my ...," expostulated the young man. "Mama! It is Art! Have you no soul? No! How can an ordinary person imagine what's it's like? You see the end before you like a shining beacon on a distant hill, and just as you are about to reach it, you ...."

"You propose marriage to my daughter and fill her ears full of nonsense about your brilliant future!" Mr. Manchester completed the sentence.

Roland turned an astonished eye upon their visitor. "What? What's that you say? Who are you? What do you know of it?"

"I, you jackanapes, am Aurora Manchester's father. What do you have to say to that?"

"Whose father?"

"Aurora's — the young lady you asked to marry you last night at Lady Jersey's rout."

"Marry me? Lady Jersey's rout? No! Did I? Oh, wait a minute! You mean that lovely girl in the flowing gown? My Diana?"

"Her name is Aurora and she's not your Diana or anything else. If you think I would allow my daughter to ally herself with a ... a ...." Mr. Manchester seemed to have no words to describe what the young man in front of him was.

"A Poet!" said Roland proudly. "You may not have heard of me yet but as soon as my play is finished and my Diana takes the main role, the world will hear of me."

"Roland, look at me!" his mother spoke with steel in her voice. "Did you, in fact, ask this girl to marry you?"

The young man reluctantly turned towards her. "No! Well, yes, I suppose I may have. But only because I need her for my play. She is Diana! I must have her! And I knew all the old tabbies would think it improper unless we were married. That's all. It's quite simple."

"SIMPLE? roared Mr. Manchester. "Simple, is it, to stand there and have the effrontery to tell me you asked my daughter to marry you so that you could put her in some damned play? You must be mad! Well, let me tell you at once, my lad, she will not marry you. She will not be your Diana, she will not be in your or any other play as long as I'm alive to prevent it! I absolutely forbid it! A cub like you? A... a... POET?!" If the young man had announced he was the offspring of Lucifer himself, this last word could not have been pronounced with more horror.

"Oh, Roland, you didn't!" Lady Westcott clasped her hands together and looked at him with exasperation. "When you know perfectly well you've been promised to Marion Underwood since you were born!"

"But, Mama, Marion could never be my Diana! She's not the right sort at all!"

Mr. Manchester turned to leave. "I have my answer and you have yours," he said. "If this Marion will have him, Lady Westcott, you should jump at it. You will be lucky to find any woman to take him. Your boy appears to be dicked in the nob. He should be locked away. I wish you good day!"

With that, he bowed and was gone.

2

"Oh, Papa, you didn't!" Aurora Manchester unconsciously echoed Lady Westcott an hour earlier. "Poor Roland! I know he asked me to marry him, but, as I told you, it didn't mean anything. I don't know why you went rampaging off to Westcott House like that."

Aurora Manchester was an exceedingly pretty girl of a little under average height, with hair like a raven's wing and sparkling brown eyes set under a pair of finely shaped eyebrows. Her complexion, which owed nothing to crushed strawberries or Denmark Lotion, was remarkably fine. One admirer had called it the most beautiful sight in England.

"I did what any father would do when his daughter tells him a complete good-for-nothing has offered for her. I set him straight."

"He's not a complete good-for-nothing, actually, Papa. His fortune is considerable, though it's tied up until he's thirty. And his play *might* be quite good. He says if I play Diana it's bound to be a success."

"Listen to me, Aurora! Good play or not, you will not be Diana. You will not marry that young fool, be he rich enough to buy an abbey. It's my belief he's dicked in the nob. Mad," he added in case she didn't understand. "Anyway, you have no need of his money. Your mother left you a handsome inheritance, as you well know. You will come into it when you are twenty-one. Next year."

"Or get married, Papa. Don't forget I can access my fortune when I marry. But never mind all that. What did you think of Lady Westcott?"

"Who?"

"Roland's mama, of course! Honestly, Papa, sometimes I think you must be blind!"

"I wasn't too blind to notice she was a good-looking woman, if that's what you mean. Very good-looking. Well preserved."

"I thought so too, when I saw her at Lady Jersey's. Much better than those women you typically frequent."

"And what, my girl, do you know about the women I typically frequent?"

"I know they're all not much older than me. Really, Papa, it's time you settled down. I won't be here forever, you know. And you would be hopeless living alone."

Ignoring the last part of that remark, her father answered, "What do you mean, not here forever. Where are you going?"

"Well, I'm bound to get married sooner or later. Sooner, I expect."

"To that Westcott idiot?"

"Perhaps."

"Over my dead body."

"Even over your alive body, Papa dearest. You know when I am twenty-one I may do what I like. Mama trusted me enough to write her Will that way."

"But Aurora! Throw yourself away on that young fool? It's beyond all reason! A lovely girl like you! You could have anyone you want!"

"Well, we'll see. But let's not argue, dearest. You know it gives you indigestion. A man of your age must be careful. Anyway, I must be off to change. We're invited to the Binghams' tonight, don't forget. Go put on your new coat. How delightful it will be to enter the room on the arm of the handsomest man in the place!"

"Minx!" said her father fondly.

But as his valet put the final touches to his ensemble he found himself thinking about what she had said. He supposed she would marry soon — not to Roland Westcott, if he could do anything to prevent it, but to someone. He found it hard to imagine their home without her cheerful laughter and the endless parade of friends she seemed to attract. Would he be happy living alone? On the other hand, would he be happy living with anyone else? Her words "a man of your age" rankled somewhat, but he knew she was right. And he *was* inclined to indigestion if something upset him. Dammit.

3

Entering the ballroom at the Binghams' that night, both father and daughter were on the look-out. Mr. Manchester was determined to keep an eye on young Westcott, if he was there, but Aurora's quarry was quite different. She had it from her best friend Joanne that Anthony Wales would be there.

Joanne's father had removed the family to their place in the country for the shooting and Aurora had been there for the weekend about a month ago when Anthony had shown up, invited by Joanne's brother. He looked exactly like the hero from one of Mrs. Radcliffe's novels. He was tall and broad-shouldered, with dark curly hair and bright blue eyes. He had spent all day shooting but when she was asked to play the pianoforte in the drawing room after dinner he had volunteered to turn the pages for her. Feeling his warm breath on the nape of her neck as he reached over to do so gave her a thrill she had never experienced before. And once or twice his hand had met hers as they riffled though the music. Usually never at a loss for words, she found it hard to know how to begin talking to him.

"Have you lived all your life in the country, Mr. Wales?" she had ventured finally.

"By no means," he had answered. "I've just returned from Vienna. I'm assistant secretary to Lord Clancarty at the Congress. But I've been spending a few weeks with my mother and sisters in Buckinghamshire."

From this, she deduced that his father was no longer with them and he was the head of the family.

"I imagine Vienna was very gay?" she hazarded. She had no idea at all of what it might have been like.

"At first, not very, because of all the work that had to be done. Once Bonaparte was dealt with, though, it was better. There were all sorts of celebrations. But I think you would have enjoyed it in any case."

"What makes you say that?" she looked up at him.

"You seem like the sort of person who brings gaiety with her," he smiled at her and his eyes grew dark. "I think you would brighten even the gloomiest of places."

Then there was a cry for Aurora to play a few dances, and she was forced to oblige. One had to sing, or play, for one's supper, after all. Anthony disappeared to partner Joanne, then the other ladies of the party. The evening ended before she had a chance of a further tête à tête with him, then he was off shooting again the next day.

She interrogated Joanne about his situation. Joanne talked to her brother and learned he was the only son of a landowner who had mortgaged his lands to pay his debts. He and Anthony had become friends at Oxford, but after graduation his friend had urgently needed to earn a living. Apparently he was very good at European languages and had been offered a post in Paris with the Earl of Cathcart at the time of Bonaparte's exile on Elba. Then, when Cathcart went to Russia, Anthony had been engaged by Lord Clancarty in Vienna, where he had remained until the Battle of Waterloo put a real end to the era of Napoleon. He'd been away from home for nearly three years. It was just luck that the two had run into each other at another friend's home a couple of weeks before.

The tradition of the house didn't allow dancing, cards, or music on Sundays, and after dinner people had more or less gone their separate ways. Aurora had run Anthony to ground in the library.

"I thought I might find you here," she said boldly. "I was told you were bookish."

"Yes, I suppose I am, though I had hoped for a dance with you. I thought there must be someone else who could play the piano. But I didn't realize people were still so stuffy about Sundays. It's not that way on the Continent, I can tell you."

"Nor here, in London," she said, then added, "I would have liked to dance with you."

"Do you waltz?"

"Not very well."

He had stood up when she came in and now put his arm around her waist. He took her left hand, and humming a familiar waltz tune, danced with her there in the library.

Aurora's heart rushed into her throat and to her immense dismay, she stumbled over his feet.

"Oh! I'm so sorry! I did tell you ...."

But before she could finish her sentence, the library door opened and Joanne came in. "Oh, there you are, Aurora," she said. "Come on! You too, Anthony. I've prevailed on Mama to let us play spillikins. It's childish, I know, but anything's better than sitting around reading!"

The rest of the evening passed without a moment for private conversation. It was unnecessary, anyway. Aurora knew she was in love.

4

During the course of the ball at the Bingham's, Mr. Manchester was infuriated to see that Roland Westcott buttonholed Aurora every chance he could. As prescribed by convention, he signed his name on her card for only two dances, but instead of dancing, spent both of them with her on a small sofa, talking earnestly. Then, whenever she appeared momentarily free he would run up and press her into a corner, still talking all the time. A tall, dark-haired man joined them more than once. Who he was, Mr. Manchester had no idea. Another damned poet, probably. He saw Aurora waltzing with him later, and was glad Westcott hadn't signed his name for a waltz. The idea of that young fool with his arm around Aurora made him grind his teeth.

During the moments he wasn't watching over his daughter, the anxious papa found his eyes wandering towards Lady Westcott. Her figure was excellent and her pale pink gown with the lace overdress suited her to perfection. She never seemed without a partner and danced even the most complicated cotillions without looking at her feet. He realized he had been intemperate in his speech earlier in the day and thought he should try to explain. He finally approached her to ask for any dance she might have left on her card. He considered that the best way into her good graces.

"I'm surprised you should ask, Mr. Manchester," she said, "after our altercation this afternoon."

"I may have been too heated, dear lady," he replied, "for which I beg your forgiveness. But you like the match no more than I do. There must be something we can do about it."

"My experience with my son tells me that the less one says the better. He is presently full of ideas for a play on a Roman theme. Last week it was a medieval scene with knights and ladies that captured his imagination. Next week it will be something else. He is unfortunately, or perhaps fortunately in this instance, unable to stick to anything. He has been much indulged, I'm afraid, my husband having died when he was so young. But he is a good boy and will come around in time. My advice is for us to let it all die a natural death. Your daughter is doing the right thing by just letting him talk himself out. She seems most sensible."

"Yes, she is, generally. But do you really think so? About the proposal, I mean? It will end in nothing? The thing is, she comes into her fortune next year and will be able to please herself. It's such a worry."

"I am convinced of it. But I understand how hard it must be for a man to raise a girl alone, as hard as for a woman to raise a boy. One is inclined to be too strict, or too lenient, or worse, vacillate between the two. Truly, one needs two parents for such a task. But you asked me for a dance! As it happens, Lord Kirkbride just informed me he is forced to leave early. His wife has the migraine. She is a martyr to them, poor thing. We are old friends and often dance together when she is not in spirits enough to dance herself. But it means the waltz he had signed for is now free. If you would like to take his place, I would happily partner you. It will be the last dance of the evening, other than the Sir Roger de Coverley, of course."

"Madam, I cannot tell you how you have relieved my mind," said Mr. Manchester, bowing over her hand. "It will be an honor to dance the last waltz with you."

He was, indeed, so relieved that he went into the card room and spent the last hour of the ball there. He missed seeing Aurora approached once more by young Roland, but if he had heard their conversation, he would have known her ladyship had been right.

"I've been thinking," said the Poet. "There should be fighting in my play. It's too tame if I just have goddesses talking all the time."

"Oh, I do so agree," Aurora urged him on. "In fact, I think a little goddess goes a long way. Gentlemen with knives or swords wearing togas would be much more exciting."

"What about … what about the slaying of Julius Caesar?" Roland eyes were bright with anticipation. "I know Shakespeare has done it, but I think I can do it better. Caesar can say something really important and meaningful. All that *Et Tu, Brute* stuff is really too feeble! What's it supposed to mean, anyway? And Shakespeare didn't have blood, you know. We can have a concealed bowl of paint or something, so when the daggers are pulled out, they drip red!"

Aurora clapped her hands. "How thrilling! The females in the audience will scream!"

"But," said her swain, suddenly anxious , "how do you feel about foregoing the part of Diana? I shouldn't like you to be disappointed."

"If it's for Art, I willingly give up the role," she replied. "Your work is the important thing."

"Yes! Yes!" Roland stood up. "Do you mind if I go to the library and jot down a few ideas? I don't mean to abandon you, mind."

"You aren't abandoning me, Roland. You are embracing your Muse."

Mr. Manchester also missed seeing the tall, dark-haired man take the Poet's place on the sofa.

"Has the great artist gone?" said Anthony, "I thought he'd never leave you alone. I can't see your father anywhere either. Every time I turned around he was watching us. Is it possible he's given up?"

"Entirely possible. In any case, he wasn't watching out for you. In fact, I doubt he even noticed you. You see, my father, like so many men, can only think of one thing at a time. So I made sure he had something else to think about."

"It's better that I know no details," he said, taking her hands, "but I can see you are the perfect wife for a diplomat."

"Which diplomat is that?" asked Aurora, demurely.

"We'll see," he said, then changed the subject. "You saved the last waltz for me, I hope?"

"Yes, though your toes may never recover if I dance it with you."

"My heart will never recover if you don't," he smiled down at her and his eyes darkened as they had at the piano. "But I'd best leave you now before the matrons notice my particular attentions."

"Oh the old tabbies! They are always gossiping about something!"

"That's why we need diplomacy," he replied. "I'll be back for the waltz."

5

While the attentions of Mr. Wales to Miss Manchester may have been of temporary interest to the matrons, those of her father to Lady Westcott far exceeded it. It all began with that famous last waltz. The handsome gentleman presented himself to the lovely lady and they began to dance elegantly, neither of them worrying about their toes. They were seen to be talking with total absorption in each other.

"By Jove," said Mr. Manchester, "you were perfectly right. I believe the young jackanapes has already abandoned Aurora."

"I'd be pleased if you remembered that's my son you're talking about, Mr. Manchester! Yes, he does seem to already have another bee in his bonnet. But have you noticed the new bee in your daughter's, if I may put it that way?"

"What do you mean?" Mr. Manchester was never at his best with metaphor.

"She seems quite taken with Anthony Wales."

"Anthony Who?" Mr. Manchester looked around and spied his daughter dancing with the tall dark-haired gentleman. "Oh, him. Don't know him. Another poet, I suppose. I saw him with your boy and Aurora."

"No, you saw him trying to separate my boy from Aurora. And he's no poet. He's on Clancarty's staff. Been in Vienna this last year. The word is, his property is all mortgaged, but he's on the rise."

For Lady Westcott had not wasted her time at the ball. She had seen Anthony and made it her business to find out everything she could about him. The matrons of the *ton* were better than any newspaper when it came to people one really wanted to know about. Someone always knew someone who knew someone who knew something.

"Hmm … well, he'll have to do better than that if he asks to pay his addresses!"

"Mr. Manchester, it's high time you stopped worrying about your daughter. We've agreed she's a sensible girl. Now, tell me, when's the last time you went to the Opera?"

This question obviously led to an invitation, and one invitation to another, and that led to more private interviews, until one day Mr. Manchester approached his daughter, his color high and his voice uncertain.

"Ahem, Aurora, my dear," he began, "you cannot be unaware that Mariah and I, that is to say, Lady Westcott and I have … have … been somewhat in each other's company these last weeks. And I have to tell you, I … I …."

"Asked her to marry you!" completed Aurora, throwing her arms around his neck. "Oh, Papa, I'm so glad! It's just as I planned! I knew if you got to know her you would find her a perfect match. Much, much better than all those silly girls!"

Ignoring the last part of that remark, he said, "What do you mean, planned?"

"When I told you about Roland's proposal, of course. He didn't have an idea in his head about it until I started talking about Diana. I knew he'd want me to play her and he'd have to ask me to marry him. Or, at least, I'd have to let him know he had to ask me. Indirectly, of course. He had no notion. But what I really wanted was for you to meet his mama. Oh, Papa, you can't really believe I ever had any intention of marrying Roland!"

She said this with such a hoot of laughter that her father was too ashamed of his own foolishness to be angry with her. He just embraced her and said, "I don't think I've ever estimated you at your true worth, my dear. I hope we can find a husband for you who does."

Of course, Aurora had hatched another plan at the same time, having to do with diverting her Papa's attention away from a certain tall dark-haired man with no fortune, but who did, she thought, estimate her at her true worth. But she wasn't going to admit to that. Ever.

The Manchester/Westcott union, which had for some weeks been the subject of eager betting in the Clubs, took place a short time later, for, as Lady Westcott so sensibly remarked, at their age time was of the essence. The couple disappeared for a month onto the Continent, during which time Aurora went to stay with her friend Joanne, now returned to the capital.

Anthony had told her at their last meeting that he had to return to Vienna. He did not offer her marriage, and made no promises except that he would be back for her. She must believe in him and be patient. She had begged him to send her letters under cover of writing to Joanne's brother, but he had said such subterfuge was both repugnant to him personally and inadmissible in his position. If he wrote, it would be to her directly and openly, and moreover, he would write first to her father. She was glad then she hadn't told him any more about her scheme of misdirection involving Roland Westcott. He might not appreciate her ideas of diplomacy.

6

The days and weeks dragged by. In some ways, Anthony became almost a dream. He had been in her life for so short a time. But her heart ached for him. Aurora understood what the poets meant by the pain of love. Why hadn't Roland written about that? Clearly, because he didn't know it. Then, just a few days after the newlyweds' return, her father came bustling into the drawing room, where she was attempting, inexpertly, to cover a screen. He was waving a letter in his hand.

"My dear," he said. "I have today received the most extraordinary letter. It's from a man by the name of Anthony Wales, whom I have never met in my life. You know him though, you sly thing! Listen!"

> *Vienna, the thirtieth of October, 1815*
> *Dear Mr. Manchester,*
>
> *I have not had the pleasure of making your acquaintance, and you will therefore be astonished at receiving this letter from me. Please allow me to explain:*
>
> *I met your daughter Aurora at a house party three months ago and was immediately struck not only by her beauty, which is considerable, but by her kindness and intelligence.*

"There, my dear, what do you think of that? Hm?"

*I was lucky enough to encounter her a few weeks
later at a ball given by the Binghams. Perhaps you
observed me there. I saw at once she was being
importuned by a foolish fellow who talked of nothing
but Romans, togas, and the goddess Diana. Heaven
knows why he thought that would entertain her. She
was at length relieved of the burden of his presence
(I don't know how) and I was able to dance a waltz
with her. During our whole intercourse I was more
and more persuaded that my initial appreciation of
her had been correct. She is not only beautiful, but
clever and kind. Who else would have put up with
that prosing fellow?*

"We know, don't we, why you did it? It was all for my sake.
He's right about how kind you are!"

*Before I left her that night I had formed the desire
to ask her to be my wife. But, my dear sir, I could not
do so without the means to support her in an
appropriate fashion.*

*The truth is, my father left us with little more
than mortgaged estates. But I was lucky enough to
obtain a position with the Earl of Cathcart in Paris
and then with Lord Clancarty in Vienna. He was, as
you probably know, chief British representative at
the Congress after Lord Castlereagh's return to
England. I have been extremely fortunate in being
preferred by his lordship, who is now taking up the
position of Ambassador in Amsterdam and has
asked me to go with him, as Envoy.*

"Envoy, Aurora! That's a very senior position!"

Over the past two years, with my salary and the help of a very good estate manager, I have been able to discharge the mortgages entered into by my father. I confidently expect the estates to continue to prosper. My salary as Envoy is generous. My man of business will send details at your request. I therefore sincerely hope you will allow me to pay my addresses to your daughter.

If, as I most urgently desire, you approve my request, may I ask you to give the enclosed letter to Aurora. I have not yet asked her to be my wife, not wishing to do so without your permission. I want to do so without further delay. I think I know her feelings and I hope she knows mine. I tell you here plainly that I love her with all my heart. I know she will make me a perfect wife, both now, and I hope, when I obtain an Embassy of my own. In addition to the qualities I have already enumerated, she is the consummate diplomat.

Yours most sincerely,
Anthony Richard Wales III

"He's right, Aurora" cried her father. "The consummate diplomat! That's you!"

A notice appeared in *The Gazette* two months later:

Aurora Jane,
only daughter of
Mr. Archibald Manchester and the late Suzanna Manchester,
and
Anthony Michael Wales III,
only son of
the late Anthony Michael Wales II and Amabel Lucy Wales,
were joined in holy matrimony in a private ceremony
on the eighth of November 1815.
The couple is residing in Vienna.

The End

Love by Correspondence

Cartwright House, London
The sixth of May, 1817

Dear Miss Horton:

I am writing to apologise for my clumsiness at Lady March's ball last evening. It was inexcusable of me to tear the hem of your gown by treading on it during the waltz. I hope it is able to be repaired, and I beg you to send me the bill.

Sincerely,
Gervase Cartwright

Hans Square, London
The sixth of May, 1817

Dear Lord Cartwright,

I was not at all surprised when you barged into me and my partner last night. You have always been a clumsy brute. Besides, no doubt you were too fascinated by your dancing partner, the Lovely Cynthia Burrows, to pay attention to anything else. My maid mended the dress so there is no bill.

Sincerely,
Margaret Horton

Cartwright House, London
The seventh of May, 1817

Dear Miss Horton,

I suppose it was too much to expect you to accept my apologies in the spirit in which they were offered, that is to say, with genuine regret. It was a very pretty gown.

Yes, Miss Burrows is fascinating. But if I was momentarily inattentive to what I was doing, it was because of my surprise at seeing you there. I had thought you still in Switzerland.

Sincerely,
Gervase Cartwright

Hans Square, London
The seventh of May, 1817

Dear Lord Cartwright,

You have never expressed regret for anything you did to me in your life, as you and I both know.

As you have so intelligently guessed, I have returned from Switzerland and the finishing school. I am now in London for the season. I hope not to see too much of you. Or the Lovely Cynthia Burrows.

Sincerely,
Margaret Horton

Cartwright House, London
The eighth of May, 1817

Dear Miss Horton,

I see that though finishing school may have furnished you with some graces — you looked very well in that pretty gown — it has not improved your manners. I cannot imagine why you should wish to avoid either me or Miss Cynthia Burrows. You seem to mistrust my motives, though for what reason, I cannot fathom. But that is no reason to dismiss *her* so rudely. She is charming.

Yours etc.,
Gervase

Hans Square, London
The eighth of May, 1817

Dear Lord Cartwright,

I do not intend to use your Christian name and do not give you leave to use mine. I fear your memory must be fading. How sad! I am twenty and you are only three years older, are you not? Alas that one so young should so soon be losing his mind. But that is clearly the case, if you do not know why I mistrust you. Surely you remember carrying off my boots and leaving me on the far bank of that murky stream, so that to get back I had to wade barefoot through things I could not see. I still shiver at the feeling of I don't know what brushing against my skin. And I cut my toe on a rock. All you did was laugh and call me a scaredy cat. I told you I hated you then and I still do.

Most definitely NOT yours,
Margaret Horton

Cartwright House, London
The ninth of May, 1817

Dear Margaret,

That was nine years ago! I admit it was not very handsome of me to carry off your boots, but it was only for a joke and I did give them back. And I ripped up my handkerchief to bind up your toe. The housekeeper told my Mama I had deliberately torn my handkerchief and I got a dressing-down for it, I can tell you. Anyway, it was your fault because you kicked me when I tried to help you down from that apple tree. People don't like being kicked, especially when they're trying to help.

Yours,
Gervase

Hans Square, London
The ninth of May, 1817

Dear Lord Cartwright,

DO NOT call me Margaret. I only give my friends the right to do so and you are not one of them. I kicked you because you were standing too close and if I had tried to get down from the tree you would have seen my petticoats. My Mama had just finished reading me a lecture about letting gentlemen see them. I am a lady, after all.

Sincerely,
Margaret Horton

Cartwright House, London
The tenth of May, 1817

Dear Maggie,

See, I am not calling you Margaret. What a bouncer! I had seen your petticoats scores of times! And very dirty they were, too. You kicked me because you have always had the most fearful temper. It goes with that carroty hair of yours. It was because I climbed higher in the tree than you and got better apples. But I don't still hold a grudge against you because of the kick, so I don't know why you should hold one against me because of the boots. And you call yourself a lady? You are acting like a child.

Yours with a very good memory indeed,
Gervase

Hans Square, London
The tenth of May, 1817

Dear Lord Cartwright,

You MAY NOT call me Maggie either! And I DO NOT have carroty hair. I'll have you know, my admirers have called it Titian. I do call myself a lady, but you are certainly no gentleman.

Sincere only in my dislike of you,
Margaret Horton

Cartwright House, London
The thirteenth of May, 1817

Dear Carroty,

Admirers? I suppose you mean the Boring Bernard Wallace. You were dancing with him when I tore your gown and then again last evening when I arrived at the Davis's ball. I noticed you not noticing me. The way you put your nose in the air was really quite amusing. You should do it more often. Why did you rush out of the room when you saw me approaching? Was it because you didn't want to apologise for kicking me? Or were you afraid the BBW might ask you to dance again?

Your friend with a very good memory,
Gervase

Hans Square, London
The thirteenth of May, 1817

Dear Lord Cartwright,

Oh, were you there? I didn't see you, so obviously I didn't rush out of the room to avoid you. Really, you do have the quaintest notions! Unlike you, Bernard Wallace is most completely a gentleman. He never calls one by rude names relating to one's hair.

By the way, yours is nowadays in the most perfect disorder. I don't remember it being so when we were younger. It must take you ages to achieve the look, or perhaps you have a coiffeur permanently on your staff. Does the LCB admire it? I'm sure she does, along with your perfectly fitting coats and elegantly tied neckcloths. Really, one wonders how such a wonderful piece of manhood could have remained unmarried all these years. Perhaps, like me, others perceive beneath all this glamour the grubby boy you used to be.

Yours with an excellent memory, too,
Margaret Horton

Cartwright House, London
The fourteenth of May, 1817

Dear Maggie,

I'm gratified my appearance has caused you to *not* notice me. I cannot say the same. I have noticed *you*. Indeed, with your superior height and *titian* hair, it would be impossible not to. When did you grow so tall? It must have been while you were away at school. Does the BBW mind that you are just a shade taller than he? But I daresay he wishes for a commanding wife. His mama has ordered him around his whole life, so it's what he's used to.

Miss Burrows has never commented upon my appearance. She is too much of a lady to do so, unlike others I could name.

I do not employ a *coiffeur,* but if you wish I could find one and send him to you to tame those curls of yours. I remember them when I was a grubby boy, as you put it. They would get caught in bushes and I would have to untangle you. That's how we got caught that time by Smithers after we'd been eating the strawberries from his beds. We were lying in the grass looking up at the sky and never heard him coming. I got a beating for that. I bet you didn't, and it was all your fault. I would have got away if I hadn't stopped to deal with your hair. And then you ran off without looking back. I've never been able to eat strawberries since without an uncomfortable feeling in my posterior.

Your strawberry-stealing friend,
Gervase

Hans Square, London
The sixteenth of May, 1817

Dear Gervase,

I didn't know you'd been caught and beaten for the strawberries. You must have taken all the blame yourself, as I never heard anything about it. I didn't see much of you after that. Mama decided to send me to stay with Grandmama in Bath. I had to go to that Young Ladies' Academy there, supposedly to try to turn me into a Lady. And you went back to Eton. We didn't see each other anymore. Until you ripped my dress at that Ball the other week. Typical!

And I am NOT taller than Bernard. I think he's going to propose, by the way.

Sorry about the beating,
Maggie

Cartwright House, London
The first of July, 1817

Dear Miss Horton,

Please accept my congratulations on your engagement to Bernard Wallace. I hope you will be very happy.

Sincerely,
Gervase Cartwright

Hans Square, London
The tenth of July, 1817

Dear Lord Cartwright,

Thank you for your kind words. I understand congratulations are in order for you, too. I'm sure Miss Burrows will fill the role of Lady Cartwright to perfection and be an ornament to your House.

Sincerely,
Margaret Horton

Hans Square, London
The fifteenth of July, 1817

Mr. and Mrs. Arthur Horton request the pleasure of
The Lord Gervase Cartwright's presence
at the wedding of their daughter
Margaret June
and
Mr. Bernard Algernon Wallace,
to be celebrated at St. George's Church, Hanover Square,
London,
at eleven o'clock in the morning
on Friday the thirtieth of August, 1817.

Cartwright House, London
The twenty-sixth of August 1817

To: Mr. and Mrs. Arthur Horton.

Gervase Cartwright regrets to inform you that he will be unable to attend the celebration of your daughter's wedding. He finds that pressure of business takes him from London more than he desires.

Please convey to the couple his best wishes for their every happiness.

Gervase Cartwright

Hans Square, London
The twenty-seventh of August, 1817

Dear Gervase:

What on earth do you mean, pressure of business? What nonsense!

Maggie

Cartwright House, London
The thirty-first of August, 1817

Dear Maggie,

So! You left him at the altar! At first I couldn't believe it, but then I could believe it only too well. I remembered the Strawberry Affair. You left me, too. But bravo! I never thought he was the man for you.

I'm afraid you are the object of no end of gossip in Mayfair. I am tamping it down where I can, saying exactly what I just did: he was not for you. Or rather, you were not for him. It was like wedding a butterfly to a slug. Where are you? You've disappeared. Again.

Your friend,
Gervase

The Grange, Harefield, Middlesex
The tenth of September, 1817

Dear Gervase,

I only just received your letter. I didn't leave you! I've already told you I didn't know about the strawberry affair! You can't compare it to my wedding, or non-wedding! Anyway, why weren't you there? What nonsense was that about pressure of business? You didn't answer my note.

If you had been there, you could have seen me fly from the church door with my veil blowing behind me. It was dramatic, just like in a novel. Luckily, Timothy coachman has known me practically from birth and when I leaped in the carriage telling him to whip up the horses and be quick about it, he did. I drove straight home to the country and hid in my room until Mama arrived the next day.

She is FURIOUS and talks of sending me back to Grandmama in Bath.

I don't know about butterflies and slugs — Mama tells me I shall be an old maid and wither away and die, and the worms will consume me. I say they'll consume me anyway, whether I'm an old maid or not, but she seems to think they work more quickly on virginal flesh.

Anyway, I do not return to London this season, or maybe ever. I am in disgrace. You should be pleased. You always thought I was a disgrace, didn't you?

Your soon-to-be-worm-fodder friend,
Maggie Horton (not Wallace, thank God!)

Cartwright House, London
The fifteenth of September, 1817

Dear Maggie,

I have never thought you a disgrace.

Yours,
Gervase

The Grange, Harefield, Middlesex
The twentieth of September, 1817

Dear Gervase,

You are the only person alive who doesn't.

I found out you were at home here last week but nobody was allowed to tell me. Why? Did they think I would lead you into scrapes like I used to? I was the one who wanted to climb the apple tree and steal the strawberries, you know I was.

I also found out the reason they gave for sending me to Bath after the Strawberry Affair. Cook let it slip one day when I was in the kitchen "helping". That means eating bread and jam while she does all the work. She's old now but remembers those days. I always used to go down to the kitchens when I was in trouble, which was often!

For once, your Mama and mine actually spoke to each other and agreed about something. It was that we should be separated. I was eleven, so you must have been fourteen. Apparently they agreed it wasn't proper for a boy and a girl of our ages to be alone together so much. But I think the real reason is our families hated each other.

Everything seemed to happen all at once that summer. I went to live in Bath, I became a woman (if you understand me) and I went to school a month later. It's funny, I don't remember missing you very much. Did you miss me?

Yours,
Maggie

Cartwright House, London
The twenty-fifth of September, 1817

Dear Maggie,

Yes, I did. Very much.

Gervase

The Grange, Harefield, Middlesex
The thirtieth of September, 1817

Dear Gervase,

I heard your Papa has been ill and is no longer able to get about the way he did. I'm sorry for that, though I know he never liked me, any more than my Papa liked you. You know he hated your father because of that business over the Lower Meadow. He always maintained it was rightfully ours and never approved of me associating with you. He died complaining about the perfidy of the Cartwrights. And your father once described me in my hearing as "that damned hoyden". Sorry about my language, but everyone already thinks the worst of me, so it can't make any difference.

I suppose this means you will be coming back here more often to run the estate?

As for me, they are sending me back to Grandmama's. They say it's because she is getting frail and needs my help. Grandmama has never been frail in her life! I think it's because they don't want me here when you bring your bride home. Do they think I'll make you climb trees again?

But, really, I don't mind Bath, to tell you the truth. There's more to do there than here, with the Assemblies and concerts and everything. Perhaps I shall find a husband! He'll probably be about seventy and suffer from the gout, but then he'll die and I shall be a merry widow. That would be fine! You've no idea how hard it is to be a single woman in disgrace with no money of her own!

When exactly is your wedding? I haven't seen a date anywhere.

Your friend,
Maggie

Grosvenor Square, London
The fifteenth of December, 1817

The Honorable and Mrs. Forsythe Burrows
request the pleasure of Miss Margaret Horton's presence
at the nuptial celebration of their daughter
Miss Cynthia Ann Burrows
and
Lord Gervase Andrew Cartwright
on the sixth day of February, 1818
at eleven o'clock in the morning
at St. George's Church, Hanover Square, London

Milsom Street, Bath
The third of January 1818

To: The Honorable and Mrs. Forsythe Burrows.

Miss Margaret Horton regrets that she will be unable to attend the nuptial celebration of their daughter Cynthia and the Lord Gervase Cartwright. She will be needed in Bath to care for her aged grandmother.

Please convey to the happy couple her best wishes for their future happiness.

Margaret Horton

Cartwright House, London
The sixth of January, 1818

Dear Maggie,

How can you refuse an invitation so far ahead? Anyway, you told me your Grandmama doesn't need your care.

Gervase

Milsom Street, Bath
The eleventh of January, 1818

Dear Gervase,

Why should I travel all the way to London in the middle of winter to see you wedded to the LCB? Besides, you know the sixth of February is my birthday. My twenty-first birthday! I shall at last be free!

You told me Bernard was not the man for me, and the LCB isn't the woman for you. Don't they call her The Icicle? No wonder she wants to be married in February.

You never used to like the cold. I remember having to hug you to keep you warm that day in the winter before the Strawberry Affair. You'd run away from home without your coat. I wanted to give you mine because I'm never cold, but you said you damned well (sorry, language again!) weren't going to wear a girl's coat, no matter how cold it was. Why did you run away from home? You never did tell me.

Your friend, the Old Lady's Companion,
Maggie

Cartwright House, London
The seventeenth of January, 1818

Dear Maggie,

I ran away from home because my father had accused me of
not being a man and preferring to play with girls. I was bookish,
as you know, and when I wasn't reading I spent most of my time
with you. That's why I didn't accept your coat. But it was nice of
you to offer me it and I shouldn't have been so churlish.

Your cold friend,
Gervase

Milsom Street, Bath
The twenty-third of January, 1818

Dear Gervase,

*Is it true the Icicle has broken it off? Mama arrived yesterday.
I knew something momentous must have happened as she hates
to travel in the winter. I heard her talking about it to Grandmama
as I crept down the stairs. I've taken to creeping because they
won't talk in front of me. But I heard Mama say she wasn't
surprised. No woman in her right mind would marry a Cartwright.
Then she said Grandmama was not to mention it to me When I
went into the salon they fell completely silent. That's why I have
to be very good at creeping.*

*Of course, they don't know we write to each other. My maid
bribed the postman (well, I did really!) to give your letters only to
her directly and she makes sure he gets mine to you. How
ridiculous for a grown woman to have to stoop to such*

subterfuge. But I'll be twenty-one next month and then I shall do what I like!

I'll wager you aren't in disgrace like me over the failure of your engagement! Men can get away with anything!

Your friend with many questions,
Maggie

Cartwright Hall, Middlesex
The twenty-eighth of January, 1818

Dear Maggie,

Yes, It is true. My betrothal is at an end. I'm sorry to say my fiancée discovered the pile of letters from you that I had been re-reading just before she came in. She had been staying here since Christmas. I can't imagine how I came to be so careless as to leave them out. She accused me of carrying on a clandestine correspondence with you. That was foolish, as I told her. There was nothing clandestine about it, as witness the fact the letters were lying there in plain view. She demanded our communication come to an end immediately.

When I refused, saying you are my oldest friend, she said she was tired of hearing your name. According to her, I talk about you all the time and even some of the older servants have told her stories of our scrapes when we were children. They seem to hold you in great affection. Finally, she threw first the ring then all the letters in my face and left, declaring our engagement at an end. I've never seen her so passionate.

No, I am not in disgrace. Such a thing is impossible for the *de facto* head of the family which I now am. Papa barely knows what is happening these days and spends most of his time nodding in front of the fire. I suppose I should be more filial, but he was unkind to me as a child and I find it hard to be sorry for him now. Mama tried to remonstrate with me, but I told her my marriage, or lack of it, was my own affair.

I find the severe shock to my system from recent events has made a cure necessary. I am coming to Bath to drink the waters. I shall call on you at eleven o'clock in the morning next Friday, the fifth of February. No nonsense from you, Miss Horton. I expect you to be at home.

Yours,
Gervase

Milsom Street, Bath
The fifth of February, 1818

Dear Gervase,

I was waiting at the top of the stairs for you to pull the bell this morning and when Paulson opened the door to you I wanted to fly into your arms. I was so happy to see you! But I suppose I've finally become the Lady they've tried so hard to make me. Then when you proposed we take a walk, I said it wasn't proper to go without a maid as chaperone. How stupid! When we were children we crawled on our bellies under the bushes together!

The thing is, I suddenly felt so shy. I didn't know what to say to you. Isn't it silly, when I've been able to say absolutely everything in my letters. I wanted to tell you that the years fell away the moment I saw you at the ball last May. I wanted to tell you I've thought about you every minute since you ripped the flounce on my gown. I wanted to tell you I only became betrothed to the BBW because I thought you were going to marry the LCB. I wanted to tell you all that, and all I did was talk about the cold weather we've been having. I could tell you were disappointed, but you were too much of a gentleman to push me further.

Come back, Gervase. Come back, please.

Your stupid friend,
Maggie

Carlton House Hotel, Bath
The fifth of February, 1817

Dearest Maggie,

And I must tell you I tore your gown deliberately back in May to have an excuse to write to you. You were resolutely ignoring me. I only asked the LCB to marry me because you had become engaged to the BBW. You've no idea how I've tried to get her to cry off ever since. I delayed the wedding date as long as I could and then deliberately chose your birthday. Leaving the letters lying about was clever, though, wasn't it?

But enough of all these games. Maggie, I've loved you all my life. I would have killed the BBW before I let him marry you. Pack a bag. I'm coming for you tomorrow morning at ten. It will be your twenty-first birthday and, as you said, you may do what you like. I can tell you, you won't be returning as Margaret Horton.

No questions, no discussions.

Yours as I have always been,
Gervase

Milsom Street, Bath
The fifth of February, 1817

Dearest Gervase,

And I've loved you all my life. I'll be ready, my darling. I'll be ready.

Maggie

The London Gazette

The eighth of February, 1818

Lord Gervase Cartwright is pleased to announce that Miss Margaret Horton became his wife on the sixth of February in a private ceremony.

The couple are traveling in Europe and will take up their residence in the country when they return.

They may be found either up the old apple tree or raiding the strawberry beds.

The Face of an Angel

1

"No, I'm sorry, Miss, er, Fellowes, I really don't think we could employ a woman." Mr. Browne, junior partner of Browne and Browne, booksellers and newsagents of 112 Paternoster Row, London, looked apologetically at the very pretty young lady in front of him.

"Women *shop* here, don't they?"

"Yes, but …."

"And do you have a salesperson who knows what women want?"

"Well, not specifically, but …."

"Then it seems to me you do need a female to wait on them! A lady customer is far more likely to ask me for guidance when it comes to certain … sensitive issues, I'm sure you agree."

"But we sell rather few of that type of thing."

"Precisely! Because a woman wouldn't ask a man to guide her to where it might be found."

"But their husbands …."

"You don't mean to tell me *their husbands* come to you asking for books about female complaints! That I simply do not believe! Gentlemen are much too squeamish about such things!"

"I should give in, old man, if I were you." A new voice added itself to the discussion.

Both Mr. Browne and the young lady turned to face its owner. He was a tall gentleman impeccably turned out and neat as a pin. His fitted coat proclaimed its origins as one of the exclusive gentleman's tailors in Bond Street. His slightly waving brown hair was brushed forward into the Brutus, a style known to Miss Fellowes because her younger brother home from Eton a few weeks ago had spent hours trying to perfect it. Simon would have admired the gentleman's neckcloth too. It was fortunate for him that his godfather had taken on the charge of his education, as they certainly could not have afforded it otherwise. But Annie sometimes wondered if this was not leading him to set his sights a bit too high. He had insisted he must have a number of these foot-wide muslin neckcloths, and had then severely tried his sister's and his aunt's patience by attempting just such a fold as this gentleman wore so effortlessly. This had resulted in him impatiently throwing to the floor half a dozen of the long cloths that then needed re-ironing.

"Mr. Rockingham!" said Mr. Browne. "I'm sorry if I've kept you waiting. Miss er, Fellowes is just leaving."

"No I wasn't!" said Miss Fellowes.

"You haven't kept me waiting," The gentleman smiled at her, and she couldn't help smiling back. "I only came in for the Racing Gazette, but I couldn't help overhearing your conversation. But the lady is right. Have *you* ever shopped for anything of a personal nature for Mrs. Browne?"

"N ... no."

"There you are then. Besides," and here he bowed in her direction, "Miss Fellowes' face would surely attract more gentlemen shoppers than any of the other assistants in here."

He looked around the huge bookstore. There were two clerks who, with their rusty-black coats and old fashioned knee britches looked at least fifty years old, and two very much younger ones whose attempts to ape high fashion, like those of her brother Simon, were less than successful.

"If I were you, I'd let her have a try. I know I'd come in more often if I knew she was here."

With that, Mr. Rockingham bowed again and was gone.

Mr. Browne looked at the young lady and sighed. It was true. She was lovely.

"Very well, I'll give you a three-month trial. If there is an increase in sales of books of special interest to women we will see about making the position permanent."

"And the wages?"

"I am prepared to pay you ten shillings a week."

"Is that the wage of the gentlemen who work here?"

"No, but you surely do not expect to be paid as much as a man?"

"For the same job, certainly I do! How much do they earn?"

"Well, I, er ...."

"I am quite prepared to inform Mr. Rockingham you tried to take advantage of me in the matter of wages."

This was quite untrue. In fact, Miss Fellowes had no idea what his direction might be and in any case, it was impossible for a single lady to write to a gentleman without a formal introduction.

Mr. Browne sighed again. "Very well. I shall pay you thirteen shillings a week for the three month trial period. If you are satisfactory, I shall raise it to fifteen shillings, which is the wage of the junior clerks here."

"And how long do they remain juniors?"

"That is hard to say. It depends upon the retirement of the older gentlemen."

Miss Fellowes rightly surmised that having learned the trade, the younger clerks quite soon tired of the endless wait for promotion and left for greener pastures. The turnover must be frequent. But she was patient. They wouldn't get rid of her so easily. She held out her hand. Her gloves were clean, but darned. "That will be satisfactory. Thank you, Mr. Browne. You will not regret this, I promise."

Mr. Browne reluctantly took her hand and was surprised at the firmness of the grip. It seemed entirely at odds with the loveliness of her face.

"At what time do you wish me to arrive tomorrow morning?"

"We open at ten, but we like the staff to be here half an hour early to make sure all is in order for the day."

"I'll be here."

2

Annie Fellowes put her bonnet and cloak on the coat rack and ran upstairs. She threw open the door to the sitting room and announced "I did it!"

"Did what, my dear?" asked an apple-cheeked lady sitting by the fire mending stockings.

"Got the job, Aunt. In Browne & Browne's. The bookstore. You remember."

"I remember you reading something about a job, but I had no idea you were thinking of applying for it. Surely they were looking for a gentleman. It can't be an appropriate position for a lady?"

"Well, Mr. Browne junior didn't think so either at first, but he was made to see the error of his ways."

"You mean your face charmed him into it."

"Not at all. I just pointed out the advantages of a female assistant to help female customers. You must remember how embarrassed you were when you had to ask the chemist for that unguent that time. In fact, you never would have got it if his wife hadn't understood the problem and stepped in."

"Yes, dear. But that was a medical issue."

"And some of the books on the shelves deal with medical issues. I was looking at one while I was waiting for Mr. Browne. It was called *Common Female Ailments and their Cures.* The Table of Contents alone was enough to make one's hair stand on end. *Inversion of the Nipples, Stoppage of the Rectum after Childbirth, The Bloody Flux.* What woman would go up to a man and whisper those words in his ear?"

Her aunt covered her ears. "Stop! Annie, stop! It isn't seemly."

"How can you say so, Aunt, when it's obvious women suffer from these things? Why should we not talk about them amongst ourselves? I'm not saying we should introduce the problem of inverted nipples at a dinner party, but quietly, woman to woman, there can be no harm. Indeed it would do us all a great deal of good."

Her aunt shook her head and said, "How a girl with the face of an angel like you should have a head full of such things I don't know."

"Unfortunately, Aunt, my face doesn't put food on the table."

"It would, if you'd accept one or other of the offers of marriage you've had."

"You want me to marry Mr. Perry, with his enormous Adam's apple and stammer? Or Mr. Rush with his belly and his whiskers?"

"Mr. Perry is a worthy young man. He can't help his Adam's apple and he only stammers when he's nervous."

"Then I must make him very nervous, for he always stammers when he speaks to me. How can I marry a man who's afraid of me? And I suppose you'll tell me Mr. Perry is worthy, too?"

"Yes, and he is very well-off."

"But I'm afraid if it was a choice between supporting us and paying for his dinner, the dinner would win. Besides, I could not be married to such a stout gentleman. He is as wide as he is tall! He makes me laugh every time I see him, and not in a companionable way!"

"Mr. Dukes is very handsome, and he seems much taken with you. You would be a fine-looking pair."

"He is not nearly as taken with me as he is with himself. Why, he cannot pass a mirror without looking in it! No, I'm sorry Aunt, but I would rather get a job and support us than be the wife of any of these gentlemen. My hope is that Simon will marry a woman of means and our problems will be over."

"He's certainly handsome enough. You must be the best-looking brother and sister in London. It is kind of his godfather to have taken charge of his education. Mrs. Westover's school was very good for you, but it would not have done for Simon."

"No indeed! She would have been too charmed by him to make him see to his studies. He has no turn for scholarship. Luckily, I did. I owe my love of reading to her."

"I just wish we could have afforded to give you a proper coming out. I feel sure some lord would have taken a shine to you, as lovely as you are."

"Thank you, Aunt. But I'm sure we shall manage without any lords. That reminds me though. An obviously wealthy gentleman intervened on my behalf at the bookstore. He helped persuade Mr. Browne to take me on. He said he'd come in more often if I were there. Perhaps he will, and fall in love with me!" She laughed merrily. "Wouldn't that be funny?"

3

Annie Fellowes was waiting at the bookstore when one of the older clerks arrived to open it the next morning.

"I'm Rufus Waring," he said. "Head clerk. I was told to expect you. You're bright and early!"

"You can tell Mr. Browne I'm keen as mustard," she said, as he led her into the store.

He showed her where to hang up her cloak and bonnet, then explained her first job would be to put away the books left out by the customers the evening before.

"We are all eager to get home at the end of the day," he said, and since we're not very busy before eleven there's time to do that job in the morning."

He showed her how a small penciled number inside each book cover indicated the bookcase it belonged in. "Then it is alphabetical by title."

"One of your jobs will be to patrol the shop and make sure customers are not spending hours reading books that they should be purchasing. It is a problem with a certain class of society."

"You mean the class that likes to read but cannot afford books?" A cloud covered Annie's features. She belonged in that class herself and had been guilty of doing exactly what Mr. Waring described.

"I'm afraid so, yes."

"Hmm …." She made no response, having already decided that customers like her should be afforded leeway.

Annie was happy putting the books away. It enabled her both to see where everything was and have a chance to look through each volume before putting it away. Once or twice she became so involved in what she was reading, she committed the sin Mr. Waring had been complaining about. She jumped when she heard his warning voice, "Miss Fellowes, I said shelve, not read!"

She soon understood the system and was a little surprised that volumes were invariably shelved by title rather than by author. In fact, when she was putting away Byron's *Hours of Idleness* under H instead of B she wondered how many purchasers would even know that's what the title was, whereas everyone knew the name of the poet. She mentioned that to Mr. Waring. He smiled knowingly and tapped his nose.

"Ah, that's where we come in, Miss Fellowes! Between us, the clerks know who wrote everything and are able to guide customers to the appropriate spot and stand next to them while they look. They are much more likely to buy that way."

4

About noon she went looking for Mr. Waring to ask about a notation she found hard to read.

"He's having a cup of tea and a bite to eat in the back," said one of the juniors. "The seniors go first, then us. We bring our own lunch but the tea's provided. For what it's worth! The scullery maid makes it for them and we get what's left. Either stewed or practically all water!"

Annie's turn for lunch came last, of course, and when she entered the dark rooms at the back of the shop, she was shocked by the appearance of the place. It was exceedingly untidy and far from providing a comfortable place for a much-needed break. A number of mismatched chairs loaded with tattered books stood around the room. The floor was littered with more ragged books, torn sheets of brown paper, straw, and string. To one side was an old table with a couple of chairs drawn up to it. Dirty cups and plates were piled on top, together with a big brown teapot. The rest of the surface was heaped with more packaging and books with twisted spines or no covers, or both.

Annie had brought a piece of her aunt's pie with her for lunch and was dearly in need of a cup of tea. She felt the outside of the teapot; it was barely warm. Then she lifted the lid and saw a pile of sodden leaves in the bottom. No drinkable tea. Anyway, she could not sit in that disorder. With a sigh, she replaced the teapot lid, cleared the dirty plates off the table and walked with them into the scullery that lay beyond. In there, every surface seemed covered with dirty crockery. A painfully thin girl in a very dirty pinafore was sitting on a stool by the hearth, rocking and singing tunelessly to herself. A huge black kettle hung above the center of the small fire.

"Hello! Is there hot water in that kettle?" asked Annie in a friendly fashion.

The girl looked at her with the vacant eyes of a person who didn't understand.

"Don't know," she said.

Annie's eyes searched for a piece of linen she could fold and use to lift the hot kettle handle, but found none. She looked around, then lifted her skirt, took up the end of her petticoat, folded it and lifted the kettle off its hook. Black greasy smears immediately discolored the white cotton, but she ignored them. Nothing a good scrub wouldn't clean. She opened the top of the kettle. In its black depths she could see simmering water.

"Is the pump in the yard?"

"Yess'm."

"Is there is a bucket?"

"Yess'm." Then she added, as if surprised she knew, "There's two."

"Then fill one about halfway and the other full, and bring them in here. Do you hear? One halfway, one full."

The girl nodded and disappeared through the back door.

Annie took the kettle into the back room and poured some boiling water first into the teapot. Then, having swept all the litter from the table on to the floor, she poured some onto the surface of the table itself. Using a piece of brown wrapping paper and some straw, she cleaned it as best she could. She took the kettle and the soiled packaging back to the kitchen. She threw the latter onto the fire then, as the girl had returned with the buckets, poured the rest of the hot water into the half-filled one. She used some of the water from the second bucket to refill the kettle, and then said to the girl,

"Wash a cup and plate in the warm water. Rinse them in there." She indicated the second bucket. "Then give them to me."

While the girl was performing this chore, Annie went into the other room and brought back sheets of the wrapping paper. When the girl gave her the two clean items, she said, "What's your name?"

"Molly, Miss."

"Well, thank you, Molly, you did a very good job. Now please do the same with all the crockery in the kitchen. Wash and rinse it. Just like these. She held up her cup and plate. Put it on the floor on these pieces of paper. I'll be back in minute to look at it all."

Molly was accustomed to being told she was stupid and good for nothing. She only had the job there because her mother told Mr. Browne that to get her off the streets she'd work for free. All she'd been asked to do was light the fire in the morning and put the kettle over it. She'd never before been told she'd done anything well in her life. And this lady that just told her so looked like an angel come down from heaven. So, her tongue sticking out of her mouth, she willingly washed crockery as she'd never washed anything, including herself, in her life before.

Meanwhile, Annie poured herself a cup of tea and unwrapped her pie onto the plate. Then she broke it in half. She sat and drank her tea and ate her pie, then poured another cup. It was weak but hot and not unpleasant. Taking occasional sips of the second cup, she organized the room. She stacked all the tattered books along one wall. There had to be more than a hundred of them. She was just picking up the wrapping paper when Mr. Browne walked in. He usually came to the shop after lunch at his club. He looked startled to see her.

"Ah! Miss, er, Fellowes! Tidying up a bit, I see!"

"Yes. I had to. How anyone could eat in here is beyond me. And the scullery! It's not fit for animals."

"Well, I, er, of course, Molly doesn't, er isn't …."

"You mean she doesn't know what to do? But have you ever told her? Given her any direction? She seems willing enough."

"No, I didn't think … Her mother … I don't …," Mr. Browne felt cornered.

Annie thought she should rescue him. He was her employer, and it was her first day.

"I understand. As a man, you are not familiar with training servants. You thought her mother would do it. Let me explain: you, the employer, always have to tell them what to do. If they are intelligent, they will do as you say but usually not a jot more. Who would willingly do extra work? If you find they have time on their hands, you must direct them to other tasks. If, like poor Molly, they are not very bright, you must explain precisely what their duties are and correct them, kindly, if they make mistakes. Molly is very willing to work if you tell her what to do. Either way, it is the employer's responsibility to get done what he or she wants, not the servant's. Or their mother's," she added.

Mr. Browne nodded. What this extraordinary young woman said made a lot of sense. Then his eyes fell on her cup of tea.

"Is there any hot tea? There usually isn't by now."

"Yes. It's drinkable but not very good. If you permit, Mr. Browne, I shall make the tea for everyone in future. And I must have a word about the sugar bowl. It's disgusting. The gentlemen's mothers must never have told them to use a dry spoon to serve the sugar and a different one to stir it. But Molly will have washed the cups by now, so if you fetch a clean one, I'll pour you a cup. Oh, please bring two. I'd like to give Molly some, too."

Mr. Browne went into the scullery to see Molly kneeling on the floor singing her tuneless song, surrounded by an ocean of clean crockery.

"Ah! Molly! My goodness! What a lot of washing up!"

Molly had started when her employer came in. He'd never actually spoken to her before. Her mother had told her to say nothing but "Yes, sir," and "No, sir," and she was wondering which one to use, when he bent down and selected two clean cups.

"Miss Fellowes wishes to give you a cup of tea," he said. "Why don't you come and get it?"

She didn't quite understand the first part of the sentence. No one had ever given her anything she hadn't had to grab for herself. But she did understand about coming to get it. She scrambled to her feet and followed Mr. Browne into the other room.

Annie poured them both a cup of tea and sweetened it, using the dreadfully sticky sugar spoon. Thankfully, she herself didn't take sugar.

"Sit and eat this piece of pie and drink your tea, Molly," she said. "You deserve a break the same as everyone else."

Molly couldn't believe it. She looked from the one to the other before grabbing the pie and gobbling it down as if they might take it from her. That had, in fact, been her experience at home with three older brothers. Then she drank her tea in one gulp.

"Well," smiled Annie. We'll work on your manners tomorrow. But for now, please bring in all the clean crockery from the floor and stack it on the table. Now, do we have a broom somewhere?"

By now, Molly would have gone on her knees to Billingsgate for the angel lady. "In the yard, Miss," she said eagerly.

"Good. After the crockery I want you to sweep the straw from this floor into a pile. We'll make packages of paper and straw for kindling. Pick up the string and roll it into a ball."

Molly ran off and Annie turned to her employer.

"Where does all this packaging come from?" She gestured around the room.

"From the cases of new books," said Mr. Browne. "We unpack and mark them in here, then put them on the shelves. Unfortunately, the packaging is often left as you see it. The junior clerks are meant to pick it up, but ...."

"No one has given them exact instructions ... or directions to take their dirty plates through to the scullery, either. May I ask you to tell them to come in here before they leave for the night? We can explain how things are to be done in future. As compensation, you may say I shall arrange it so everyone gets hot tea."

Mr. Browne stared. This woman was impossible to refuse. She stood there, with a face like an angel, telling him what to do, and all he could do was nod.

"And why are all these tattered books here?"

"Over the years we've had the opportunity to purchase books from various homes in and around the capital. When one does so, one is forced to take the good with the bad. I can't sell them in that condition, so they end up in here. I keep thinking I should do something with them but …."

No one has given you any direction either, thought Annie. Then an idea began to form in her head. She said nothing, however, and spent the rest of the afternoon making straw packages with Molly, and instructing her how to clean the floors. Then they tackled the scullery. There proved to be shelves under the débris. They were liberally strewn with mouse droppings, but once washed with hot water looked serviceable enough for the crockery to be stored there.

"We need a cat," announced Annie. A good mouser."

"At 'ome, th' woman next door's 'ad a litter of kittens few weeks back. There's cats all over."

"Good. Bring one, no, two if they're only young. The mice might be bigger than they are. Besides they'll be company for each other. Now, you saw how we bundled up the wrapping paper and straw. You are to do that whenever there's a delivery. I'll try to get the men to leave the paper, string, and straw in neat piles. You use the bundles for kindling, before adding the coal. Make sure you use the old ones first or we'll have mice nesting in them. Now, tell me back what I told you."

"I's goin' to make bundles wiv th' straw 'n paper an' use 'em fer kindlin', old ones first."

"Yes, very good. And you'll boil up a full kettle of water every day, and bring in two extra buckets of water just like you did today. The men will bring in their cups and plates and you will wash them up. Then you will use the rinse water to mop the floor, just like today, except I'll bring in a real mop, not brown paper. All of this is to be done *every day*! Now, what did I say?"

"I's to boil a full kettle o' water, and bring in two buckets extra like t'day and do the washin' up an' mop the floor w' the rinse water. An' it's every day."

"Perfect! You've done a good day's work, Molly. I'm proud of you!"

When Annie went back into the shop, Mr. Smith told her Mr. Rockingham had been in and had asked after her.

"Oh!" Annie didn't know why she was so disappointed to have missed him. He probably just wanted to see whether his opinion had carried weight. He couldn't really be interested in her. He was a wealthy man, a member of the *ton*, and it was obvious that she was not. She should be glad he hadn't seen her today. Her gown was dusty and her hair was falling down. But she couldn't help asking, "What did he say?"

"He bought the racing paper as usual and said he had expected to see you. He asked if I hadn't engaged you after all. I told him you were working in the back and were too busy to come out." He looked at her gown and hair. "I thought you would have no wish to be seen in your ... condition."

"No. You were quite right. I wouldn't."

110

Still, for the rest of the afternoon and evening she had to repeatedly tell herself to stop being so silly. Mr. Rockingham couldn't possibly be interested in her. He was just being kind. As he would to a stray dog. Probably.

5

Though the other clerks grumbled at the directions given them via Mr. Browne, everyone enjoyed the more salubrious dining environment, and especially the hot tea. Annie knew that by dint of using enough tea in the beginning, with the judicious addition of boiling water, one could have good, strong, hot tea for everyone. The day after the great clean-up she brought in a bunch of daffodils, for the spring flowers were arriving in the capital, and their cheerful color made even the scratched old table look better.

Two young cats arrived in the scullery and spent their nights to such advantage that rows of half-eaten dead mice greeted Molly when she arrived in the morning. They felt entitled to spend their days sleeping in the sun that pooled on the scullery floor once the mullioned windows were cleaned of their century of accumulated dirt. Annie showed Molly how to clean glass with newspaper and vinegar. The girl was amazed, less at the dirt, which she was used to, than at the brilliant shine. Having done the kitchen, she asked if she could do the shop windows, too.

With Annie bringing her lunch every day and praising her for her work, Molly had never been so happy. She knew what she had to do and did it willingly. She was proud of her little empire in the kitchen. But more was to come. Annie told her aunt about the poor scullery maid who worked for nothing and owned nothing but the filthy rags on her back. She would have given her a gown from her own wardrobe, as limited as it was, but she was quite tall and well developed. Neglect and malnutrition had made Molly undersized and thin. Her clothes would swamp the poor girl. But a lifetime of thrift had made her aunt keep every scrap of clothing anyone had ever worn. She found a couple of Annie's old dresses and petticoats from when she was a girl and refurbished them. Annie gave them to Molly, together with a much-darned pinafore. This was too large, but the fact that it had to be wrapped around her body twice was thought to be a good thing: it would protect the dresses all the better.

"And if you wash it out at night and hang it near the hearth, it'll be clean and dry in the morning. Look, put it here, and only here. No closer to the fire. We don't want to burn the place down!"

Molly was speechless. No one had ever given her anything before. She couldn't even remember where the garments she wore had come from. She'd always had them. Mutely, she kissed Annie's hands.

The presentation of these treasures happened early in the morning just after opening. Then Annie quietly locked the staff dining room door and the door to the yard.

"It's not much good putting on clean clothes if you yourself aren't clean," she said seriously to the girl. "I know you will think I am a madwoman, but I want you to take off all your clothes and wash yourself just like you wash the cups and plates."

Such was Molly's adoration of Annie that she stripped off without another word. Her poor, thin body, the ribs and backbone clearly outlined, made Annie catch her breath. But she showed no sign of ill treatment. No bruises or marks.

"I brought you a towel, a cloth, and a piece of soap. You do the front and I'll do the back. Stand on your old clothes. We'll probably have to throw them away, anyway."

Between the two of them, the ablutions were quickly administered and Molly was toweled dry. She stepped into one of her new dresses and wrapped the pinafore around twice. Her feet went back into her wooden clogs.

"That's much better," said Annie. "You must do it twice a week at least. If you come early and lock the doors no one will disturb you. I shall leave you the towel and the soap." Then she looked at the girl's hair. It was pulled back into an untidy bun, thin and lank. It was impossible to tell what color it was. "When did you last wash your hair?"

"I ain't never washed me 'air, Miss."

Annie drew in her breath. "Then today's the day," she said. "Luckily, you don't have a lot of hair. It won't take long. We'll need to use more of the hot water, though, so we'd better hurry, so the kettle can boil again before the gentlemen need their tea."

Before long, Molly was sitting in the sun with the kittens on her knee, drying her hair. The color turned out to be an unremarkable brown, but it waved prettily. With her fresh clothes and clean hair neatly tied back, Annie thought that with a kind housekeeper to give her direction, the girl could be useful in any household. She just wished she knew someone who needed a maid.

6

Having dealt for the moment with the problem of Molly, Annie returned to her chores in the shop, all the while turning over a plan to deal with the piles of tattered books still lining the wall in the staff dining room. She had been looking at them. Some of them were written in Latin and Greek (at least, she thought that's what it was) and were incomprehensible to her. Mrs. Westover's education hadn't gone that far. There were several tattered copies of a book entitled *A Shorte Introduction of Grammar* that appeared to be an explanation of Latin grammar, with what looked like schoolboy scratchings in the margins. There were also a number of equally ragged copies of what she only recognized as the poetry of Virgil because the poet's name appeared on the front page. There were copies of books from the previous century: *The Life of Samuel Johnson* by his friend James Boswell, Volume One of the famous *The Voyage of the Beagle* by Charles Darwin, *The Leviathan* by Thomas Hobbes, Gibbon's *Decline and Fall of the Roman Empire* (volumes I, III and V only), Daniel Defoe's *Robinson Crusoe*, Jonathan Swift's *Gulliver's Travels*, Samuel Richardson's *Pamela*, and Henry Fielding's *Tom Jones*. Then there was the poetry of Shelley and Byron, and finally the romances: the works of Eliza Hayworth, Frances Burney, Horace Walpole, Ann Radcliffe and the most recent, Jane Austen.

All the books were in bad condition, the covers defaced or torn. But the interiors, though sometimes tattered, were legible. In fact, she had begun reading *Sense and Sensibility* and could hardly put it down when her lunch time was over. She did not like to take it with her, although it was true that piled against the wall in the back room, the books seemed little more than rubbish.

She was in the middle of these contemplations when she heard a cultured voice saying her name.

"Miss Fellowes!"

She turned and was confronted by Mr. Rockingham. He was as immaculately turned out as before. She was glad he hadn't seen her the other day in all her mess.

"You appear to be lost in thought. I hope you aren't neglecting your duties. I should surely be blamed for supporting your candidacy for the position!"

She smiled. "No, though I am perhaps not the most perfect employee in terms of my ability to sell books. I hate following people around when they are trying to have a quiet read of something they can't afford. But I think my employer would already be sad to see me go because I make a most perfect cup of tea."

"I agree it's a far more important skill. But tell me, what were you dreaming about when I came in?"

"Well, you see, we have a large number of good books that can't be put on the shelves because of the poor condition of their covers. I'm wondering whether we couldn't pile them on a table and charge sixpence each, or perhaps less if they are particularly tattered. I feel sure people who can't afford the expensive volumes we sell would buy them. Most of them are perfectly readable, except where the mice have been at them."

"What sort of books are they?"

"Every sort. Latin grammars, volumes of history, Byron's verses, Miss Austen's funny novels. Just about everything."

To her surprise, Mr. Rockingham lifted an imperious finger and called, "I say, Browne! Can you come here a moment?"

The shop owner stopped what he was doing and immediately presented himself. He bowed. "How may I be of service to you, sir?"

"This is the thing, Browne. I need a Latin grammar for my nephew. Miss Fellowes has very helpfully shown me what you have, but, well, to tell you the truth, I don't feel like shelling out a lot of the ready for the young devil. He's already lost two copies, deliberately, I daresay, and besides, it's a book I happen to seriously dislike. Now, Miss Fellowes tells me she noticed a copy of *A Shorte Introduction of Grammar* in a pile in the back room. It's in poor condition but perfectly usable, she tells me. I wonder if I may purchase that, for say, sixpence?"

Mr. Browne looked astonished. "Miss Fellowes says we have a copy of it in the back room?"

"Yes," replied Annie. "Several. It must be the sort of thing schoolboys have and it ends up in the book collections when they take it home. I'll go and get one."

She was back in a minute with a ragged copy of the volume, which she handed to Mr. Rockingham.

"Good Lord!" he said, turning it over in his hands. "It looks exactly like the one I had at Eton. In about the same condition, too. I'm not surprised it's been ill-used. I hated it! The only good thing about it was that it was a good size to put down one's britches before being caned. I burned mine when I left. I remember. It made a fine blaze."

He reached into his pocket and produced a silver coin. "I never thought I'd see the blessed thing again," he said with a rueful smile. "It brings back unpleasant memories! But I'm most grateful to you both." He bowed and walked out of the shop with a jaunty step.

"Well!" Mr. Browne seemed at a loss for words.

Annie saw her chance. "There must be many people who either can't afford a book or who, for reasons of their own, don't want to spend too much for one. Why don't we set up a table over in the corner with the tattered volumes from the back room? We can put up a sign: *Well-Used Volumes, 6d.* We juniors can take turns watching over it."

"It is certainly an idea, Miss Fellowes, most certainly an idea. Let me talk it over with the senior clerks."

"Don't forget you will be making money out of something that is at the moment just a perfect place for mice to nest and will otherwise simply be thrown away. I've been tempted to put the lot on the fire more than once."

The senior clerks were skeptical, but agreed it was worth a try, so long as they personally did not have to deal with such inferior merchandise.

The Well-Used table turned out to be immensely successful. The lure of a bargain is always impossible to ignore. Regular customers visited it and, better still, people who generally did not frequent bookstores heard about it and came in. The ladies were the most assiduous customers. They came for the Romances, but often bought "improving" books for their sons and husbands. The more handy of them even repaired the covers and presented them as gifts. It was a mark of pride to be able to say, "Oh yes, I gave my John a book for his birthday. He has always been a famous reader." The John in question generally fell asleep of an evening with the Racing News over his face, but the refurbished book looked very well on the table.

A side-effect of the number of women visiting the shop was that Annie was frequently consulted for advice on books dealing with female complaints. It was as she had surmised. They whispered they would never have asked one of the male clerks, but could she possibly direct them to a book that might have a cure for …. Sales to women soared, and if a woman could not afford the book, Annie, who quickly became quite an expert in the contents of these specialized volumes, was able to tell her what it said. As he totted up the figures at the end of the quarter, Mr. Browne had to admit she was worth the salary increase, and more.

Mr. Rockingham was a frequent visitor. On the rare days she didn't see him, Annie had to hide her disappointment. He always had an excuse for coming in. Usually it was to buy the Racing News, but on several occasions he claimed to be looking for something else. He needed a book for a niece. No, not a Romance; his sister would not approve. Annie proposed a pretty illustrated book on the meaning of flowers. It was perfect, just what he was looking for! Then, another time he said his mother had heard Miss Austen's works were delightful, which should he buy for her? One day he picked up off the Well-Used table the incomplete set of Gibbon's *Decline and Fall of the Roman Empire*.

"But it's missing two volumes!" said Annie. "And, if you don't mind my saying so, you look as if you could afford a complete set."

"Oh, I've no intention of actually reading it. I mean, from what I remember, the Ascent of Rome was enough of a bore. The Decline and Fall must be even worse."

Annie laughed. "But in that case, why buy it at all?"

"So that I can leave these tattered, obviously often-read volumes lying around the house so my friends will admire my erudition. They think me a fellow who only reads the Sporting News."

"Aren't you?"

"Yes, but there's no need for them to think so."

"And, of course, the ladies will be impressed." It was out of Annie's mouth before she could prevent it.

"What ladies?"

"The ones who hear you've been reading Gibbon. Word is bound to get around."

"My dear Miss Fellowes," he smiled. "I assure you, if I impress any lady because she thinks I read such stuff, she is not the lady for me."

There was a moment of silence, and he looked as if he were going to say something more, but he did not, and soon after, took his leave.

7

One late afternoon on a Saturday in mid-summer, Annie asked her superiors if she could stay a little late and rearrange the Well-Used table. She had been meaning to do it all day, but had been too busy. They were not open on Sunday, of course, but she would lock up securely and arrive promptly on Monday morning to open up.

The main door to the bookstore and those inside were all propped open to allow the breeze to cool the premises down a little. By six o'clock there was no one in the shop. Molly was still in the scullery, washing out her pinafore, as Annie had directed. Annie was engaged in arranging a new pile of books on the Well-Used table when she heard a cry from the scullery.

"No, no! Get orf me! Leave me 'lone!"

She ran into the kitchen and saw a man holding Molly around her narrow waist with one hand and attempting to lift her skirts with the other. Molly was vainly trying to beat him off, but he was much bigger than her.

Without thinking, Annie ran to the struggling pair and tried to pull the man off. She got nowhere. He was broad and heavy and very strong. In desperation , she threw off his greasy cap, buried her hands in his hair and pulled as hard as she could. With a roar, he let go of Molly, turned and hit Annie across the face with such force that she flew across the room and crashed into the shelves of crockery. Cups, plates, and bowls fell all around her, one shard catching her on the neck. She slid to the ground, dazed but conscious.

Molly screamed, "Miss! Miss!"

"Scream all yer want," shouted the attacker. "I'll do you first then I'll have yer Miss."

Into this mayhem came a familiar voice. "What the devil …?" and the form of Mr. Rockingham appeared in the doorway. In what seemed less than a second, he had crossed the room, and the attacker was flying backwards into the wall. He hit his head, crumpled to a heap and lay silent.

She felt a large, firm hand in her back, he was holding her to his chest and his voice close to her said urgently, "Miss Fellowes! Are you all right? Good God, you're bleeding!"

A moment later, something soft was pressed hard into the side of her neck. Then, "Thank God, it's seems to be just a scratch. Are you able to hold this against it, while I see to the other young lady?"

"Yes," she heard herself say. "I'm fine. Just a little dazed. Please look after Molly." She put her fingers to her neck and pressed the pad she found there. When she looked at it, she saw it was a fine linen handkerchief embroidered with R in one corner.

She felt him leave, and, her senses returning fully, she heard Molly saying, "Oh, sir, thank you. I'm all right. 'E didn't get what 'e were after. But 'ow's Miss Fellowes? 'E ain't 'urt 'er, 'as he? Please tell me she ain't bad!" and she burst into tears.

Mr. Rockingham's low voice soothed her, and after a moment Annie saw him walk over to the attacker, who was still inert on the floor. He knelt and felt his pulse. "He'll live. Pity I didn't hit him harder. Is there anything I can tie him up with, Molly?

Annie answered. "There's a ball of string next to the hearth. If you double or triple it, it should be strong enough."

She watched as he turned the man onto his back and efficiently tied his hands and ankles. Then he left them, returning in a couple of minutes to say, "I've sent a link boy for the constable. He should be here soon."

Annie tried to stand up. Her head swam and she had to sit down again. "Can someone poke up the fire and put the kettle on for tea?" she said.

"I can do that, Miss," said Molly. "You stay put. 'E 'urt you more'n me. The bastard." She went over to the prostrate form and kicked it.

"One would normally say it's bad form to hit a man when he's down," said Rockingham grimly, "but in this case I'm all for it!"

Molly had just made the tea and given Annie and Rockingham a cup when the constable arrived. The attacker had come to and was attempting to roll over. Finding his hands and feet bound he bellowed.

"You quiet down, me lad," said the constable, who had taken in the scene at a glance. "I'll get to you in a minute. Now, who's going to tell me what went on here?"

The tea had cleared Annie's head. She briefly but clearly explained what had happened. The cut on her neck and the broken crockery, together with Molly's torn petticoat, was all the evidence he needed. He carefully wrote down their names and addresses, and took a stiff white card offered by Mr. Rockingham.

"Do you know the perpetrator?" he asked.

"Yes. 'E's me mum's friend, if yer knows what I mean," said Molly, her head down. "'Is name is Sam. Don't know no more 'n that. He saw me yesterday and tried to kiss me, but I ran away. 'E must 'ave found out where I work an' come 'ere to get what 'e wanted. But Miss Fellowes saved me, though 'e nearly killed 'er! Oh, Miss, I'd rather it'd bin me!" She burst into tears again.

"Right then," said the constable, evidently not wanting to deal with a crying woman. He went outside and blew his whistle. Almost immediately, two other officers appeared, had a brief conversation, and left. "They're bringing a covered cart," he explained. "He'll appear before a magistrate Monday morning. He can cool his heels in gaol till then."

An hour later, the would-be rapist had been loaded into the cart, protesting all he wanted was a little fun, and carried off. Molly had swept up the broken crockery and washed up the teacups. Her scullery was her kingdom and she was proud of it.

"I don't know what me mum's goin' ter say when I tells 'er. She'll be cross, fer sure." said Molly. "She'll prob'ly say it were all my fault fer leadin' 'im on. But I didn't! It were 'im said as 'ow I'd turned out all right an' should give 'im a kiss."

It was true. Being fed at least one meal a day, Molly had lost her starved look. She followed Annie's directions about being clean, and nowadays, with her neat clothes and hair, she looked a different person. Hearing her explanation, Annie made a decision.

"You'll come home with me tonight. I don't think you should go home, at least for today."

"But what about the cats, Miss? I gen'rally comes 'ere of a Sunday to be wiv 'em."

"Do you? I had no idea," said Annie. "But you can come tomorrow, just the same."

"In that case, I shall drive you both," said Mr. Rockingham. "I'm anxious to have someone look at that wound on your neck, Miss Fellowes. Once you are home, I shall call for the doctor."

"Oh, no!" said Annie quickly. "I can't thank you enough for what you've done already. You are truly our savior. But there's no need to drive us, or call for a doctor. We'll take a hackney."

"Certainly not! You have both suffered a dreadful shock. I should worry all night if I did not see you safely conveyed. You are doing me a service in allowing me to drive you."

What could she say? She was ashamed for him to see how meanly she and her aunt lived, and truly did not need a doctor. It was a scratch, nothing more. A little basilicum powder was all that was required. But short of rudely refusing him outright, she could do nothing.

8

Accordingly, Mr. Rockingham, whose Christian name, it turned out, was Edward, but who was invariably called Rocky by his friends, led them to his elegant phaeton waiting outside. He explained he had been driving home from an afternoon at his mother's (she loved *Pride and Prejudice*, by the way!) and had passed by in the hopes of seeing Miss Fellowes. He had seen the shop doors wide open and then heard the screams. It was the hand of Providence, they all agreed. At least, Annie and Rocky agreed, and Molly just nodded her head, unable to speak for the glory of being driven in such an elegant vehicle by the two people who figured in her mind as gods.

Annie's aunt received them all with astonishment but grace, listened to the story with horror, agreed with her niece that no doctor was required, sent Molly to the kitchen to be fed, and invited Mr. Rockingham to share their supper. He mentally sent to perdition the tonnish party he was supposed to attend and gratefully accepted.

It was, necessarily, a simple meal, but Mr. Rockingham enjoyed it more than he had enjoyed a meal in years. He was tired of the gossip that passed for conversation at the parties he usually went to; he was tired of the society ladies with their brittle laughs and cruel comments; he was tired of the subtle and not-so-subtle attempts to engage him. Miss Fellowes' lovely face had haunted his dreams for weeks, and her forthright, open demeanor enchanted him now. Her intelligent remarks, her humor and her aunt's quiet comments were music to his ears. By the time the evening was over, he was well and truly in love.

"If I may, I shall come by tomorrow afternoon to see how you go on," he said as he took his leave. "About two o'clock? Perhaps we could go for a walk?"

Annie, of course, had been in love with him for weeks. The thought of going for a walk alone with him brought a blush to her cheek. "I...I'll ask my aunt," she said. He kissed her hand, and left.

When asked whether it was proper for her to walk alone with an unattached man, her aunt, who had seen immediately which way the wind was blowing, laughed.

"I don't recall your asking me if it was proper for you to apply for a position in a shop full of men," she said.

"I know, but they're all … just men."

"And Mr. Rockingham is not just a man?"

"No. He's not. He's *the* man. I love him, Aunt."

"And there was I thinking you a modern woman! You silly girl! If you don't walk with him tomorrow and give him every opportunity and encouragement to make the proposal of marriage I'm sure he's going to make, you're a bigger fool than I take you for. It's as plain as the nose on your face he loves you, too."

And so it was. Miss Fellowes was strangely quiet as she walked with Mr. Rockingham the following afternoon, but she smiled at him so sweetly he was not discouraged.

"Miss Fellowes, Annie," he said. "I know our acquaintance has not been of the normal sort. Until yesterday I had only ever seen you at your place of employment, but please believe me when I tell you how ardently I love and admire you." (The reader may judge that his mother had not been the only one to read Jane Austen.) "Will you do me the honor of ...."

"Yes! Oh yes! I will! Oh please, thank you!" cried the lady, her face wreathed in smiles.

Rockingham roared with laughter. "But how do you know I'm not asking you to do something altogether disgraceful?"

Annie's smile vanished and her eyes widened in shock. "Are ... are you?"

"No, of course not. I want to marry you, my angel. I've wanted to ask you for weeks now, but you've always seemed so ... busy."

"Thank goodness!" said Annie. "My aunt told me to act like a modern woman, but I don't think even she would have approved of anything else."

"Nor would my mother. I told her yesterday I was going to ask you. That's why I stopped by the shop so late in the day."

They fell into each other's arms and there, to the delight or scandalized shock of passers-by, kissed until they were both breathless.

"You won't make me read Gibbon, will you?" he murmured in her ear.

"If you help me learn Latin," she murmured back.

"Oh God! If I'd known that," he said, holding her at arms' length, "I would've used the *Grammar* for more than stuffing my britches. Are you sure I can't just teach you to read the racing form?"

"We'll see."

Mr. Edward Rockingham and Miss Ann Mary Fellowes were married a month later. To the great disappointment of Mr. Browne and the clerks, the lady did not continue to work at the bookshop, though her improvements in the matter of tidiness, tea and the Well-Read table continued after her.

Molly didn't stay there either. She moved into the Rockingham residence and proved a faithful and hard-working maid until, five years later, she married the butcher's boy. He was spending so much time at the kitchen door, that the housekeeper said either he had to move in or she had to move out. Mrs. Rockingham was delighted when, a year later, Molly gave birth to a daughter. The proud new mother named her Ann Mary, in honor of the lady with the face of an angel.

The End

The Négligée

1

"I hear Esmé Fotherington is privately sporting a decidedly improper négligée," remarked Ivo Rutherford, Duke of Sarisbury, one morning to Imogen, his wife.

They were at breakfast where she had her chestnut head buried in the financial columns of the newspaper. She had not yet dressed for the day and was wearing her own pretty but modest négligée of amber silk over a cotton nightdress that covered her from neck to foot.

"That's nice, dear," came her distracted reply.

"It's apparently completely transparent apart from a froth of lace around her feet and wrists. And she wears nothing under it. At least, that's what Dickie Smythe told me last night in the club. But he may have just been trying to distract me from the cards. I was winning."

His lordship mused, a smile playing on his lips as he regarded his wife.

"It's still early and she probably doesn't rise until noon. I thought I might go and take a look. Just for the sake of verification, of course. One does like to be accurate."

"What's that?" she looked up at him at last.

"Verification. I plan on doing some."

"Of what?"

"Of what Dickie Smythe told me, as I just said."

"What did you just say?" She had the grace to look guilty. "I wasn't listening."

"I know." Her husband stood up, smiling. "Just as well, you probably wouldn't have liked it."

Now her attention was fully caught. "Ivo, you beast. Tell me what you were talking about."

"No. A man likes his wife to hang upon his every word. Not only do you not hang upon mine, you don't even know I've spoken. Anyway, I'm off. I'm fencing at noon and I think I've just enough time for verification before that, if I hurry."

He walked around the table and bent to kiss his wife's cheek. He had to bend a long way. She was rather petite and he was well over six feet tall.

"That's a very pretty négligée you're wearing," he said, as he stood up, his eyes laughing into hers. "But not a patch on Esmé's, if reports are correct. I'll let you know."

And before she could collect her wits to reply, he left the room.

Imogen sat back in her chair, her brow furrowed, wondering what all that was about. What did he mean about Esmé? What négligée? What wouldn't she like? Oh, it was just like Ivo not to explain! Then she pursed her lips. Of course, it was true she hadn't been listening to him. She certainly hadn't been hanging onto his every word. But the news about the proposed railway line extension had caught her eye and really, how was she supposed to concentrate on two things at once? Oh well, no doubt all would become clear in due course. About Esmé and the négligée, that was. The railway line extension, now that was something she'd definitely have to find out about immediately. That was important.

2

The Duke had, of course, no intention of visiting Esmé Fotherington, or any other woman. He adored his wife, even if she seemed to prefer the financial news to him. Or perhaps precisely because she did. She had never sought to capture his attention as so many women had. Long before he was married the mamas of the *ton* had given up parading their eligible daughters in front of him; he had acquired a deserved reputation for playing fast and loose with women of a quite different sort.

So when he married Imogen Mainwaring, a young and lovely widow, the *ton* was astonished. They weren't even known to be acquainted. But there they were, apparently blissfully happy. The Duke certainly hadn't looked at another woman since.

Of course, there was her money. Her late husband had left her quite a fortune, but she had since parlayed it into a vast one, investing in what most people considered new-fangled ideas. But Imogen's money meant nothing to Ivo. He had enough of his own and he wasn't going to pore over any investment reports to enlarge it. He had people to do that for him.

But Imogen did. She loved nothing more than financial statements and company prospectuses. Ivo smiled to himself as he left the house. He was proud of his wife's acumen and had never objected if she found the stock market at least as fascinating as him. But it was fun to tease her now and then. Had he given her something different to think about, he wondered? It would be entertaining to see.

It is well known that one only has to think of a person one hasn't seen in an age, for that person to suddenly appear. His fencing session over, the Duke was walking down Pall Mall thinking pleasurably about purchasing for his wife the sort of négligée he had entirely fictitiously ascribed to Esmé, when who should emerge from a fashionable linen draper's but the aforementioned lady herself.

Esmé Fotherington had briefly been his paramour years before, and it had ended in a fateful duel with her husband. But the consequence had been his meeting Imogen, and a complete change in his way of life. Esmé was still a pretty woman with generous curves, which were somewhat more generous now than five years ago.

"Ivo!" she said, with pleasure in her voice. She had always regarded him somewhat in the manner of an angler who regretted the one that got away.

"Esmé," he replied, lifting his tall beaver hat with almost equal pleasure, for a pretty woman is always a pleasant sight. "I heard you were back. And still as lovely as ever!"

"Flatterer!" She lightly tapped him on the chest with the palm of her hand, for they were, after all, old friends. "I don't know how you can say that, when you threw me over so unconscionably."

"I?" he laughed. "But you had your eye on young Andrews, as I recall."

"Oh, Digby Andrews was all right in his way, but you know …."

"And you've had no shortage since, from what I understand."

"Well, one has to pay one's bills." She stopped and looked him straight in the eye. "You aren't … in the market, so to speak?"

"No, 'fraid not." He laughed. "Old married man now, you know."

"Yes." She did know, but there was no harm in asking, after all. Her latest arrangement had come to an end. That's why she was back in town. She gave a shallow curtsey. "Well, I must be off. But you're looking well, Ivo. Marriage must agree with you,"

"It does. Oh, before you go, Esmé, tell me, if one wanted to buy a rather, let us say, inappropriate négligée, where would one go these days? I'm so out of touch with such things."

She laughed. "And to think, not so very long ago you would have been the primary source of such information! But Dushay's is where you should go. A discreet little place on Jermyn Street. They deliver in very plain brown boxes."

"How convenient! Thank you!" He smiled, lifted his hat, bowed and they parted.

3

Finishing her breakfast tea, Imogen decided to pay a visit to Martin Carter, her man of business. He would know all about the railway line extension. An hour later she was climbing into one of the carriages with which the stable was amply provided and giving the driver instructions to go to Fleet Street. The late summer was still warm, so she had chosen a light muslin day dress with all over sprigs of green. The color matched both the shawl thrown over her arm in case of draughts and the lining of a poke bonnet sitting on her shining chestnut curls. It reflected the green of her eyes. She looked charming and girlish, anything but the formidable business woman she was. A number of gentlemen had discovered this to their cost when they discounted her interest in new opportunities and then realized she'd stolen a march on them, buying a controlling share while the price was still low.

As they clip-clopped down Pall Mall, Imogen caught sight of a tall gentleman talking to a pretty lady in pink. The lady was smiling up into his face and patting his broad chest. It was a curiously intimate gesture. With a shock, she realized the tall gentleman was her husband and the pretty lady was Esmé Fotherington. Ivo had been talking about Esmé at breakfast! What had he been saying? Oh, how she wished she had been listening! But it was probably nothing. They were old friends, that's all. Ivo had never talked of the women in his life before they met, though she knew there had been several. But she couldn't help wondering now whether Esmé had been one of them.

She completed her business at the office in Fleet Street, leaving Mr. Carter somewhat bemused. Lady Sarisbury was usually absolutely on top of any issue. Today she had been rather distracted. He had to twice repeat the route the new train line was to take, and though she had nodded knowledgeably, she had asked no questions about projected passenger or freight loads or potential competition, all of which he was prepared for. It was most unlike her. He wondered what could be on her mind. She could have domestic problems, of course: a new housekeeper, a ball to arrange. He was a bachelor. His landlady did his laundry, prepared his meals, and kept his rooms clean. Apart from carrying out Lady Sarisbury's instructions and going to his Club, he did nothing. Nevertheless, he considered himself constantly busy and had no idea that Imogen, or any woman worth her salt, could do at least three things at once.

Imogen was home for luncheon and she was glad when Ivo presented himself as well.

"Hello darling," she said, nonchalantly, but surprised him by standing on tiptoe to kiss his cheek. She was enthusiastic in the bedroom but otherwise not given to displays of affection. "What have you been up to this morning?"

"Oh, you know, this and that. Fencing, went to the Club. The usual."

He kissed her by her ear, and his warm breath made her shiver. But she persevered.

"Did you see anyone different?"

"What do you mean? Different?"

"Someone you haven't seen for a while. A friend back in town, perhaps."

Ivo looked at her enquiringly. He had forgotten Esmé. "No, not that I can think of. Did you?"

"Me? No, I didn't see anything … er, anyone. I went to ask Mr. Carter about the railway extension. That's all."

"So that's what you were so engrossed in this morning! Where's it going?"

"Oh, from somewhere to somewhere."

He laughed. "You surprise me! I somehow thought it would go from nowhere to nowhere. Didn't Carter know?"

"Yes, he told me but, well, I can't remember."

Ivo was surprised again. "Are you feeling quite well? Normally you would have anticipated passenger loads, fuel costs, and the names of the chief engineers at your fingertips."

"Yes, but I didn't really pay attention."

Ivo laughed. "I'm glad I'm not the only one you don't listen to! Come on, let's have lunch. And maybe a lie-down afterwards?" He waggled his eyebrows suggestively.

He was joking, but he was surprised at the vehemence of her response.

She was thinking that if he was telling the truth about not seeing anyone different, it could only mean that seeing Esmé was a common occurrence. And that meant ... she didn't want to think what that meant.

"Don't be ridiculous!" she said quickly. "I ... I can't."

She went into lunch in silence.

Imogen didn't have a large number of female friends. She spent too much time in the City, where she was usually the only female in sight. This had never bothered her before. Now she wished she had a confidante. She wanted someone to tell her she was being silly, that her husband loved her and only her. There was her old aunt, of course, but she hardly went anywhere anymore and wouldn't know what the *on dits* were. Still, she was better than no one.

Accordingly, a day or so later she took the carriage to her aunt's house. She still lived in the pretty house by the park Imogen had leased for them both, then bought, when she first came to London.

"Imogen, my dear!" her aunt was delighted to see her. "But are you altogether well? You look tired!"

Imogen realized she had not felt really well for the last few weeks. She'd put it down to the late nights caused by the parties they'd been to. All the hostesses left in London seemed determined to offer some sort of evening *al fresco* event where nothing even began until candles were lit in the trees after nightfall, which in London at this time of the year could be past ten o'clock.

"Aunt, do you know Esmé Fotherington?" she asked without preamble.

"How odd!" replied her aunt. "That's the second time I've heard that name in a matter of days, And yet I cannot say I know the woman. That is to say, I know who she is, but we move — or moved I should say, as these days I hardly move at all — in different circles. I'm much older than she is, of course."

"What did you hear about her?"

"Well, my friend Poppy Warner was just remarking the other day that Cumberland Place was becoming quite a fashionable address. In my day it was *very* looked down upon! Nothing but cits and mushrooms! She said she'd heard Esmé Fotherington has taken a place there. But I daresay it's all she can afford. Her husband was killed, you know."

Then her aunt put her hand over her mouth. "But of course, you weren't in London when it happened!"

"When what happened?"

"When the Duke killed her husband. At least, no one believed he did it deliberately. The *on dit* was that the silly man ran onto his sword."

"The Duke? You mean Ivo?"

"Yes. Your husband. But it was all over before you ever came on the scene."

"He told me he'd accidentally killed someone and that's why he was in Switzerland when we met. But I never knew who it was."

"It was Fotherington."

"Were they fighting over *her*?"

"Evidently, though when Ivo was exonerated and came back to London I never saw them together. In fact, if I'm not mistaken, she already had another gentleman in tow. She never seems to have a shortage. Anyway, why are we raking up all that old history?"

"Oh, no reason. It's just that I saw her in town the other day. She's very pretty."

"Putting on flesh."

"But not unpleasantly."

"Yet."

"Oh Aunt, that's not very generous!"

"I'm just telling the truth. In five years she'll be a butterball."

Imogen chuckled, rather pleased with her aunt's words. Then the conversation turned to other matters. After a cup of tea and a piece of seed cake of which Imogen could hardly bear to swallow a crumb, she took her leave.

Ivo had laughed off the whole affair of the swordfight when they first met, and they had never discussed it. But he still practiced fencing very regularly and once in the early days of their marriage had even showed her how to perform a few elementary moves. She had liked the feel of the sword in her hand, and said she thought she'd like to fight with it. But Ivo had made her laugh. She was so much shorter than he, he said, that she would have to run him through the knees rather than the heart.

But if he had fought over Esmé, and then hadn't had the opportunity to pursue the affair after he came back from the Continent, perhaps he now regretted it. Had he decided to take up where he had left off? She argued with herself in the carriage all the way home. No! It couldn't be true! Ivo was exactly the same as ever, teasing and laughing, never away from home for more than a couple of hours. But he hadn't been near her in the bedroom for, what was it? A week? Or more? It was true he had made that joking suggestion at lunchtime. She shouldn't have repulsed him so definitively. Perhaps he would come tonight. Then, at an appropriate moment, she could ask him about Esmé. That was a consoling thought.

But Imogen was not the only one who was good with sums. Ivo usually knew exactly at what moment in the month his wife would not receive him. He had hoped it was over by now, but her response at lunch had indicated the opposite. "I can't," she had said. He thought he must have miscalculated, so after dinner he kissed her cheek, wished her good night, and said if she didn't object, he would go to his club for a hand of cards. Imogen's heart sank. She determined to stay awake to see what time he came home. But she was unusually weary and fell sleep almost as soon as her head touched her pillow. She would have been relieved to hear him come home only an hour later, but she didn't.

5

The following evening the Duke and Duchess were invited to a rout at Lady Pecksmith's. That lady had decided to outdo her peers by organizing a treasure hunt in the large back garden of their townhouse as night fell. Lanterns had been placed in the trees but finding the clues in the penumbra and then reading them proved a considerable challenge. People were soon stumbling around either giggling or cursing, depending on age and sex.

Needless to say, a few of the young unmarried men deliberately loitered where they could not be seen and then made a show of accidentally clasping at any eligible female who happened to pass by. The young ladies quickly caught on, and shrieks of pleasurable shock were soon heard emanating from all corners.

Imogen found little pleasure in the activity and thought she must be getting old. But then, she reflected, she never had been keen on such silliness. Perhaps it was because she had never had much opportunity for it. She had married young and her first husband had been considerably older than she. But she and Ivo joined in willingly enough this evening. He was at her side at first and proved remarkably adept at finding and interpreting the clues. But then she had lost sight of him and was wandering around with the last clue in her hand. *In the deep I can lie*, it read, *but then again be dry.* What on earth could that mean?

Going in no particular direction, she found herself looking at the fountain in the center of the garden. She was alone. The other guests seemed to be enjoying themselves in the trees and bushes. The fountain featured six large fish spouting arcs of water. *In the deep,* she suddenly thought. Fish! *But then again be dry.* She looked again, and saw that between the larger fish there were smaller ones not spouting. Their mouths were open, but nothing emerged. Dry. She cautiously put her hand in each open mouth, and on the third attempt felt a small, square box. She withdrew it and opened it. By the light of the lanterns placed all around the fountain, she saw a lovely little silver brooch in the curving profile of a fish, with a green stone for the eye. It might have been made for her! She was delighted. Perhaps these treasure hunts were fun, after all.

Just then she heard a shriek and a woman's voice laughing, "Ivo! What *are* you doing?"

"I should think it was obvious, Esmé!" came the unmistakable voice of her husband. "But …," and his voice lowered so that she could hear no more.

Imogen stood stock still, her hand gripping the little box till her knuckles were white. Her first instinct was to run towards the voices and claim her husband from that woman. But then anger boiled up in her. No! If he preferred to play silly games with her, let him!

By now others were converging on the fountain, and the word *fish!* was being repeated here and there. Someone noticed the box in her hand and called, "Look, Lady Sarisbury has the prize! What is it, Imogen? Do let us see!"

In a daze, she gave the box to an outstretched hand and heard the exclamations, *A brooch in the shape of a fish! How pretty! How clever! What a nice prize! Where was it?*

She forced herself to smile and reply, "In the mouth of one of the fish. It was quite dry. Yes, such luck!"

As soon as she could, she went into the house, took a glass of wine proffered by a footman and gulped it down. She sank into a chair, trying to control her beating heart. Other people began to move indoors looking for refreshment and a few minutes later the tall form of her husband was by her side.

"Imogen! There you are!" He smiled at her.

But before he could say any more, Daisy Vereker bustled up, holding out the brooch box and crying, "You forgot to take this, Imogen!" She laughed merrily, "I was tempted to keep it! It's so pretty!"

"Oh, did you work out the last clue? Clever girl!" Ivo looked at the fish brooch. "Very nice! Well worth my effort!"

"What do you mean, *your* effort," retorted Daisy. "Imogen worked it out, not you!"

"But I found all the clues leading to the last. Then my dear wife abandoned me, no doubt to take credit, as she is doing, for the whole!" laughed Ivo.

I abandoned him? thought Imogen. *What a convenient lie!* But the effect of this exchange was to bring her to her senses. She squared her shoulders and forced herself to smile up at them both. "Let us say we abandoned each other," she said. "Now I'm going to do it again, to thank the hostess for her generosity I'm tired, Ivo. I think we should go home. But you're right, Daisy. It is a very pretty brooch."

She rose and moved away.

6

Imogen said rather little in the carriage on the way home and Ivo didn't press her. He knew her cycles often made her feel out of sorts.

"How weary I am!" she said, as they entered the wide foyer of the Sarisbury townhouse. "I'll see you in the morning. Goodnight, Ivo." And she went straight upstairs.

Ivo was not really surprised, except about how he had so badly miscalculated the time of the month. But he gladly mounted the stairs and went to bed.

Imogen was crossing the foyer the following morning reading the headlines of the newspaper that was in her hand, when the doorbell rang. Unusually, neither the butler nor any of the footmen were there. In fact, they were all in the kitchen where an itinerant boot-seller was displaying his offerings. She knew Ivo had gone to his usual fencing exercise. It was just as well he wasn't there for though he was a generous employer, he would have been angry at this dereliction of duty.

In the event, Imogen went to the door and opened it herself. A boy in livery thrust a box into her hands with the words, "Delivery from Dushay's." In her distracted state, with the newspaper headlines still in her head, she heard this as *Delivery for the Duchess*. The boy hung around looking meaningful until she realized what he was waiting for. Then she went to the hall table, deposited the newspaper and the box, and looked in the dish where a few coppers always reposed for just such occurrences. She gave him a couple of coins and shut the door.

She picked up the box and gave it a little shake. She had no idea what it could contain. The exterior gave nothing away; it was brown and very plain and bore no marks other than the address, written quite small. She went into the family parlor and proceeded to open it, surprised to find it contained layers and layers of pink tissue paper that seemed entirely at odds with the sober appearance of the outside. Finally, to her astonishment she drew from its depths a diaphanous négligée with a froth of lace at the cuffs and around the bottom. She held it up to the light and saw it was almost totally transparent. She gasped. Who ordered this? Then she remembered Ivo's words the other day: *That's a very pretty négligée but not a patch on Esmé's.*

She sat down abruptly on the straw-colored sofa in the parlor and stared at the item in her lap. Then she picked up the top of the plain brown box and read the direction. It was written in a small, discreet hand.

> *To the Duke of Sarisbury*
> *Leicester Square*
> *By Hand from Dushay's*

The box was not addressed to her! She should not have opened it at all! She hastily re-nestled the garment back into its pink tissue, replaced the lid and carefully went to the door of the parlor. No one in the foyer. Thank goodness. She quickly placed the box on the hall table, picked up the newspaper and was on her way back to the parlor just as the butler reappeared.

"A delivery for my husband," she said, gesturing at the box. "I opened the door."

"I'm so sorry, your Grace, I left my post for a few minutes. I hope you were not inconvenienced."

"No, but I know his Grace would not like the hall to be unattended. Anyone could come in off the street. One would never know!"

"Of course, your Grace. It won't happen again." The butler hoped she wouldn't complain to the Duke. He knew how his employer felt about the front hall. With any luck, she'd forget all about it. He certainly wasn't going to mention it!

Imogen ran upstairs and fell on her bed. A négligée! And a very improper one, at that! It could not be for her! Ivo had never bought her anything like that in the past, even when they were first married. He must have bought it for that Esmé. It would be entirely appropriate for a woman like that! Oh, what was she to do?

Then she sat up with a martial light in her eye. She marched to the door that communicated with her husband's room, threw it open and looked around. There they were! She saw the long black leather cases containing Ivo's épées. She quickly took one and went back into her own room. Although the weather was a too warm for it, she took her green velvet cloak from her wardrobe and put it on, practicing walking with the sword case hiding in its folds. Then she tied her green-lined bonnet over her curls, took up her gloves and reticule and ran down the stairs.

As she made straight for the front door, the butler surged forward from his tall-backed seat and asked, "May I call for a carriage, your Grace?"

"No, I've a quick errand to make. It would take too long to pole up the horses. Find me a hackney, please."

"Are you sure, your Grace? It would only take a few minutes …."

"I'm sure. Please do as I ask."

Imogen was unusually short with him and after being absent for the package delivery, he dared not say more. So he went into the street and hailed the best-looking hackney he saw passing. He tried to help his lady up into it, but she waved him off, not wishing to reveal the long box wrapped in the folds of her cloak.

He heard her say "Cumberland Place" and wondered why the Duchess of Sarisbury should be going to such an unfashionable address. Unlike Imogen's aunt, he hadn't heard of its recent rise in desirability. Then he helplessly watched her being borne off. He didn't like it.

7

The hackney driver didn't care who he took where, so long as he was paid, but when they arrived in Cumberland Place and Imogen asked him to enquire as to where a Mrs. Esmé Fotherington might reside, he was less enthusiastic.

"I'll pay you for your trouble," said Imogen, and rummaged in her reticule to produce a silver coin, which she showed to him. Since the customary fare was only a few pence, he became immediately more amenable. Within a very few minutes, by dint of asking in the servants' quarters accessed by steps going down in the front of the tall houses, he had found out that Mrs. Esmé Fotherington lived at number 21.

"And a very nice lady she is, too, seemingly," he reported, "though there was some as said she ain't no better than she oughta be."

With this rather mixed review, he jumped up and drove her along to number 21. He showed unusual courtesy by getting down to open the carriage door for her, received his fare and the silver coin, which he bit between decidedly unclean teeth before grinning with satisfaction. Then he said, "You want as I should wait fer yer, Missus?" He had taken quite a shine to this mort, pretty as she was.

"No, thank you," replied Imogen. With the desperate deed she had in mind, she thought it was better if no one saw her emerging from number 21 Cumberland Place.

With a cheery wave, the hackney man took off, leaving her to climb the steps and pull the bell. She waited a few minutes, growing more nervous by the second, until a person who looked like a housekeeper, dressed in a very proper black gown with starched white, lace-edged collar and cuffs, opened the door.

"I am the Duchess of Sarisbury," said Imogen, feeling, as she always did, a little ridiculous with such a title. "I should like to see Mrs. Fotherington."

The woman hesitated, then said calmly, "Please step in, your Grace. May I take your cloak?"

"N … no," replied Imogen, quickly, still concealing the sword case. "I … I shan't be here long."

The woman inclined her head and led her to a small parlor off the equally small but well-proportioned entrance hall. "Please sit down. I shall just see if Mrs. Fotherington is, er, receiving visitors."

Left alone, Imogen looked around. The parlor was small, to be sure, but furnished with taste and comfort. It looked lived in. The late newspaper was lying on a small table. She was tempted to pick it up and look at the stock prices, but resisted.

The door opened and Esmé came in. "Your Grace," she said, coming forward with a smile and outstretched hands. "How comes it that we haven't met before? Ivo must be keeping you in cotton!"

Imogen didn't know how to respond. She couldn't take the other woman's hands, as she was grasping the sword case with her right hand and politeness forbade shaking with the left. She made a shallow curtsey, therefore, saying, "Mrs. Fotherington". The formality of it checked Esmé. She stopped and curtseyed herself, rather lower, before indicating a chair and saying, in a different tone, "But won't you sit down, Your Grace?"

Imogen tried to do so, but found the sword case made it almost impossible. In the carriage she had laid it on the seat. She finally backed into a chair, holding her right hand with the case stiff by her side and lowering herself. As she sank down, the case was pushed into her armpit. It was extremely uncomfortable.

Esmé looked at her curiously. "But are you quite well? Your arm? Is it injured?"

Imogen gave up the subterfuge. "No!" she said loudly, "I am not injured, but you are likely to be very soon!"

She pulled the box from under her arm, laid it in her lap and struggled with opening the straps. Esmé looked at her as if she were mad, then stood up as she realized what Imogen was doing.

"Your Grace!" she said, aghast. "Whatever can be the matter?"

By now, Imogen had freed the sword from the case and was standing up, holding it in front of her in a threatening fashion.

"Mrs. Fotherington," said Imogen wildly, "I demand you give up my husband! I shall use force if necessary!"

"Give up your husband? Do you mean Ivo?"

"Of course I mean Ivo! I've only one husband!"

"But I can't give him up! I mean," cried Esmé, running behind a chair as Imogen lunged towards her, "there's nothing to give up! He's not interested in me. I offered, but he told me he was happily married."

"Then what were you doing with him in the dark at Lady Pecksmith's the other day?"

"Lady Pecksmith's?" Esmé looked puzzled. "Oh, you mean during the treasure hunt. I wasn't doing anything with him! I didn't even know he was there until he nearly pushed me over!"

"I heard you laugh and say, 'Ivo, whatever are you doing!'"

"So would you have if a man backed into you trying to unhook a rose bush branch from around his coat button!"

"Oh," said Imogen lamely. Then she started up, waving the sword. "But what about the négligée! He bought you a completely transparent one!"

Esmé skipped back behind the chair. "He most certainly did not! All I know about a négligée is that he asked me where he could obtain one, and I told him Dushay's!"

"Oh!" said Imogen again. She lowered the sword.

"So it's not you! It must be someone else!" And she burst into tears.

Esmé came out from behind the chair and, after carefully removing the sword from Imogen's limp hand, put her arm around the sobbing woman and led to the sofa.

"Why do you think it's anybody?" she asked gently. "From what I've heard, Ivo has eyes for no one but you. Couldn't he have bought it for you?"

"For me?" Imogen sniffed and looked up, tears trembling on her long lashes. "Why would he do that?"

"Well, you know him better than I, but perhaps he wanted to give you a gift that would, let's say, encourage you in a certain direction?"

Suddenly, Imogen understood. Of course! He wanted her attention! He hadn't exactly said that, but that's what he had meant about not hanging on his every word. And she had actually rebuffed him!

"Ye ... es," she said slowly. "We haven't, well, you know, for," she calculated, "over two weeks now."

"Why not? Did you quarrel?"

"No! It's impossible to quarrel with Ivo. He just laughs at everything. Anyway, we've nothing to quarrel about!"

"So why do you think he stayed away?"

Imogen wrinkled her nose, then opened her eyes wide. "He must have believed it was not, not, you know, the right time." She stopped, then said, "And normally, he would have been right, but it wasn't. I mean, it should have been, but it wasn't."

Esmé apparently had no problem interpreting that garbled remark. "That usually means only one thing, my dear. You are increasing."

"Increasing?" Imogen was astonished, but instantly knew she must be right. That must be why she had been feeling so tired and out of sorts recently! And why she had conceived the incredible notion of attacking Esmé with a sword! She would never have done such a thing in her right mind!

"Can it affect your mind as well as your body?" she asked.

"Most certainly. Women become irrational, moody, prone to tears. All sorts of things. At least for the first three months. My sister has five children and I've seen her go through it all each time."

"You have a sister?" Imogen had never thought of Esmé as a person with a family.

"Yes. Luckily, she and her husband live in the country and never come to London. They know nothing of my ... adventures."

"I... I see," said Imogen. "I imagine that would be inconvenient."

"Yes, very," said Esmé. She smiled. "Look, your Grace ..."

Imogen stopped her. "It's hard to be formal with someone who just tried to kill you," she chuckled. "One is inclined to take that sort of thing personally! Please call me Imogen."

Esmé laughed. "Yes, indeed! And I am Esmé. How about a cup of tea, Imogen? And a nice cose. We've got lots to talk about, I think."

8

About an hour later, Imogen took her leave, the efficient housekeeper finding her a hackney and helping her up into it. It was she who had done up the straps on the sword case, which she now placed in the carriage. She had asked no questions. Imogen guessed that being in Mrs. Fotherington's employ she had to be the soul of discretion.

Ivo came into the hall when he heard her voice.

"Hello, my love," he said, and then stopped. "What on earth are you doing with my sword case?"

"Oh, this and that," she said airily. "I was thinking of taking up fencing, but then I realized it wouldn't be a good moment."

"Any moment is a good moment for learning to fence," he replied, leading her into the parlor. "But let me give you lessons. I'm as good as anyone and I want to see you in tight britches."

"I know you would be a good teacher," she said, pushing him into a chair so she could sit on his knee and put her arms around his neck. "In fact, the best. But I'm not going to have the figure for it, especially not tight britches."

"You have the perfect figure," he said, squeezing her waist.

She looked him in the eyes. "Ivo, I have something to confess. I opened that box from Dushay's. I didn't realize it was addressed to you. The négligée is for me, isn't it?"

"Of course it's for you, you goose! Who else would I buy it for?"

"Well, I did wonder. It's most improper!"

"I know." Ivo raised his eyebrows at her. "That's why I bought it."

She smiled and tightened her arms around his neck. "I'm glad you still think of me like that, Ivo. I know I've not been a very attentive wife, and I'm sorry. The négligée's lovely and I'm looking forward to wearing it. But I'm afraid it will soon have to be put away for a while. It won't really be … suitable."

"Why?" The Duke looked puzzled, then a broad grin split his face. "So that's why you've been a little out of sorts! Clever girl! What wonderful news! In that case, we'd better use it as much as we can while we can."

"Would now be convenient?" asked Imogen, sliding off his knee. "Or we could just take a look at the evening newspaper."

"Hang the newspaper!" said her husband, springing to his feet. "We've more important things to do."

A Note from the Author

If you enjoyed this novel, please leave a review! Go to the Amazon page and scroll down past all the other books Amazon wants you to buy(!) till you get to the review click. It really does help independent authors like me. Thank you so much!

A Perfect Match and Other Regency Romance Stories

A Marriage is Arranged

GL Robinson's next Regency is now on pre-order at a special price. **A Marriage is Arranged** will be live in September 2023. This story of two strong-willed people navigating the shoals of an arranged marriage will make you smile — as well as make you want to give both of them a kick in the rear! Use the QR code to access the Amazon book page.

Here is a preview:

Chapter Four

"Well, my dear! Didn't I say he would want to marry you?" cried her mother. "You are exactly the wife a man like him is looking for. You are well bred and you know not to make a fuss. But my goodness! One cannot call him good-looking. He looks, well, he looks almost like an ape! And his manners are not exactly what one expects from a gentleman. But then, he is probably accustomed to people toadying to him." She looked searchingly at her daughter. "I hope you did not find him altogether unappealing, my dear. I would never push you into marriage with a man you found repulsive."

"No, I did not find him repulsive."

She hesitated. How could she explain how her body felt one way and her mind another. She could see how proud and unmannerly he was, but she was irresistibly drawn to him.

"I must agree, though," she said with a smile, "we will make the ugliest couple in London. Our poor children will have to look further than their parents for any share of beauty. Let us hope they take after their grandmama!"

"Oh, my dear!" her mother smiled, "I can have no pretentions to beauty now, though it's true I was much admired when I was younger."

"Nonsense, Mama! You know you are still a very pretty lady. Everyone says so. I fear when I'm no longer here to frighten them off you will fall prey to hosts of suitors."

"Now you are being ridiculous! And you are not ugly! If you would only let your hair curl by your ears instead of putting them in those tight bands, you would look so much better!"

"But he offered for me as I was, with my braids and my old brown gown."

Since this was irrefutable, Mrs. Grey could not contradict her. But privately, she thought that after the wedding ceremony her daughter was going to have to do a little better if she wanted her husband to stay close to the hearth. He might be rude and look like an ape, but with his position and money there would always be women who found him attractive.

Her daughter knew what she was thinking but said nothing. She had promised their marriage would be successful, and she had meant it. She didn't know how yet, but she would arrange it.

The Earl returned the following week, having sent a note of the day and time of his arrival. On this occasion, he arrived in a carriage drawn by four beautiful bays. Entering the house, he ordered the butler to have them led to the stables. When informed of this by her startled manservant, Mrs. Grey was a little shocked, but gratified that it at least showed his intention of staying for somewhat longer.

Louise knew he had been shown into the library where her mother was waiting. She stayed in her room for a footman to come to inform her when she was wanted. He delivered the message some twenty minutes later, and she descended the stairs slowly, again clad in her brown gown, her curly hair tightly held in its bands.

The gentlemen rose when she entered, and she saw a flash of surprise in the eyes of the gentleman who must be his lordship's man of business. She understood. She must look quite different from the fashionable women in London.

"Ah, Miss Grey, there you are." The Earl did not come forward to greet her, but gave a shallow bow from where he was standing. He indicated his companion. "This is Arnold Booking. My man of business."

The solicitor did approach her; he bowed formally and murmured, "Miss Grey."

They sat at the long library table, on top of which a leather-covered box lay open and next to it an inkwell and pen. Mr. Booking pulled a chair out for Louise next to her mother. The Earl merely sat down.

"His lordship has been most generous," said Mrs. Grey.

She put a piece of paper in front of her daughter and Louise read it carefully. She had the impression her future husband was not expecting her do so, for he drew his prominent eyebrows together in a frown. He said nothing but tapped his fingers on the polished surface of the desk. To her astonishment she saw that after her marriage she was to be given the enormous sum of a thousand pounds a quarter. This was ten times more than her current allowance.

However, she did not want to appear like an excited schoolgirl being given an unexpected treat. She nodded slightly in the Earl's direction and said, "Yes. I see. Thank you."

There was a moment of silence, then Mr. Booking said, "If you would both be so kind as to sign that you have read and agree to what is laid out here?"

The Earl reached for the pen and ink, signed the document in silence, then pushed it towards her. Under his signature, which was simply the word *Shrewsbury* written in a determined hand, she wrote *Louise Mary Grey*.

The solicitor produced a ponce box and shook fine sand over the signatures.

"Now," he said, looking a little anxiously at Louise's mother and herself, "we come to the more delicate issue of his lordship's, er, conjugal rights."

Louise couldn't stop herself. "Conjugal rights?" she said in astonishment.

"Yes," said the Earl, speaking for the first time since she had sat down, "I think it best for this to be laid out so there is no misunderstanding later. It is entirely usual in France where as far as arranged marriages are concerned, these things are managed better than here."

Apparently anxious to have done with this part of the settlements, the solicitor said quickly, "His lordship proposes once a fortnight until the first child is conceived and if it is a male child, once in a thirty day period thereafter, the actual days by mutual consent."

Louise looked at her mother, who, however, refused to meet her eye.

"You must forgive me," she said quietly, feeling a blush coming to her cheek, "I had not considered this question at all. I should like to speak to my mother in private, if you please."

The Earl drew his brows together, but after a hesitation he rose, followed by his man of business. They left the room.

"Mama! Have you ever heard of such a thing?" she said in an anxious semi-whisper.

"No-o," replied her mother slowly, in the same whisper, "but you know, my dear, it is a good idea. One is otherwise in the position of constantly wondering whether one's husband is, well, going to visit one that night. That can make for, er, disagreeable uncertainty. This way, you will agree and it will be done, and you will be free for two weeks until the next time. I think many women would like that. I know I would have. Not that I didn't care for your father, you understand," she added quickly. "But it will make your life more, well, comfortable. You'll see."

"I suppose so," said Louise doubtfully, "Though since I know rather little of what is entailed, I cannot tell how I shall feel."

"Well, we can't go into all that now," said her mother hurriedly. "We cannot keep his lordship waiting. He didn't seem to want us to discuss it at all."

"His wishes concern me less than my own at this point, mama. Of course we cannot discuss it now, but please let us talk of it later."

Her mother looked even more uncomfortable but said, "Yes, yes, later, but not now."

Louise went to the library door and opened it. The two men were sitting next to each other on the straight-backed bench in the hall, for all the world like two schoolboys waiting to see the Dean. Louise's wide eyes danced with amusement at the thought.

Arnold Booking noticed them. *Why, she is not such a mouse as she appears,* he thought, *I wonder if Gary appreciates it.*

He always called the Earl *Gary* to himself. The man was so infernally superior, he liked to take him down a notch. The old Earl had been much easier to deal with. He smiled at Louise and she smiled back. *Yes, definitely not a mouse,* he decided.

They came back into the room.

Once they were seated, Louise said calmly, "I agree to that... arrangement."

Her future husband merely nodded.

His man of business produced the document and they both signed as before. Mrs. Grey invited the gentlemen to take a glass of sherry to celebrate the conclusion of their business.

"Yes, please do," said Louise quietly. "I believe the horses are stabled, so there is no danger of their taking cold."

Dammit, thought the Earl. *Does the girl miss nothing?* But he bowed in acquiescence and accepted a glass of sherry. He was surprised when it turned out to be remarkably good.

Pre-Order *A Marriage is Arranged* Now!

https://www.amazon.com/gp/product/B0BMY1WXGD

Regency Novels by GL Robinson

Please go to my Amazon Author Page for more information:

Imogen or Love and Money Lovely young widow Imogen is pursued by Lord Ivo, a well-known rake. She angrily rejects him and concentrates on continuing her late husband's business enterprises. Will she find that money is more important than love?

Cecilia or Too Tall to Love Orphaned Cecilia, too tall and too outspoken for acceptance by the *ton,* is determined to open a school for girls in London's East End slums, but is lacking funds. When Lord Tommy Allenby offers her a way out, will she get more than she bargained for?

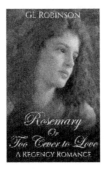

Rosemary or Too Clever to Love Governess Rosemary is forced to move with her pupil, the romantically-minded Marianne, to live with the girl's guardian, a strict gentleman with old fashioned ideas about how young women should behave. Can she save the one from her own folly and persuade the other that she isn't just a not-so-pretty face?

The Kissing Ball A collection of Regency short stories, not just for Christmas. All sorts of seasons and reasons!

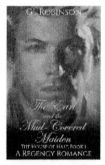

The Earl and The Mud-Covered Maiden *The House of Hale Book One*. When a handsome stranger covers her in mud driving too fast and then lies about his name, little does Sophy know her world is about to change forever. **Now free to download!**

The Earl and His Lady *The House of Hale Book Two.* Sophy and Lysander are married, but she is unused to London society and he's very proud of his family name. It's a rocky beginning for both of them.

The Earl and The Heir *The House of Hale Book Three.* The Hale family has a new heir, in the shape of Sylvester, a handful of a little boy with a lively curiosity. His mother is curious too, about her husband's past. They both get themselves in a lot of trouble.

The Lord and the Red-Headed Hornet Orphaned Amelia talks her way into a man's job as secretary to a member of the aristocracy. She's looking for a post in the Diplomatic Service for her twin brother. But he wants to join the army. And her boss goes missing on the day he is supposed to show up for a wager. Can feisty Amelia save them both?

The Lord and the Cat's Meow A love tangle between a Lord, a retired Colonel, a lovely debutante, and a fierce animal rights activist. But Horace the cat knows what he wants. He sorts it out.

**The Lord and the Bluestocking** The Marquess of Hastings is good-looking and rich but is a little odd. Nowadays he would probably be diagnosed as having Asperger's syndrome. To find a wife he scandalizes the *ton* by advertising in the newspaper. Elisabeth Maxwell is having no luck finding a publisher for her children's book and is willing to marry him to escape an overbearing stepfather. This gently amusing story introduces us to an unusual but endearing Regency couple. The question is: can they possibly co-exist, let alone find happiness?

**Heloise Says No** The lovely and mysterious Héloise Ramsay is available ... for a price. The Earl of Dexter is prepared to pay it, and more, but she refuses him. He knows she's had other lovers, so why not him? This is the story of a woman who makes a mistake in her youth, and finds that someone in her circumstances has no choice but to sell her only asset: herself.

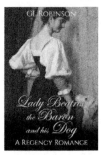

Beatrix, the Baron, and his Dog   After harrowing experiences in the Napoleonic Wars, half-English, half-German Lukas is making a home for his mother and sister in the leafy green of England. Meanwhile his sister and mother are in London, falling under the sway of Lady Beatrix, a frivolous socialite. Her thoughtlessness leads her into having to accept an offer of marriage from the strict and disapproving Lukas. The world as she knows it seems about to fall apart. But then there's Juno, Lukas's old hunting dog, who unerringly points everyone in the right direction.

About The Author

GL Robinson is a retired French professor who took to writing Regency Romances in 2018. She dedicates all her books to her sister, who died unexpectedly that year and who, like her, had a lifelong love of the genre. She remembers the two of them reading Georgette Heyer after lights out under the covers in their convent boarding school and giggling together in delicious complicity.

Brought up in the south of England, she has spent the last forty years in upstate New York with her American husband. She likes gardening, talking with her grandchildren and sitting by the fire with a good book and a nice cup of tea! She still reads Georgette Heyer.

Printed in Great Britain
by Amazon

20992787R00108